BLOOD
AND BONE

BOOKS BY TARA BROWN ALSO WRITING AS
T. L. BROWN, A. E. WATSON, ERIN LEIGH, AND SOPHIE STARR

Tara Brown

BLOOD AND BONE

Montlake
Romance

Published by Montlake Romance, Seattle

www.apub.com

Amazon, the Amazon logo, and Montlake Romance are trademarks of Amazon.com, Inc., or its affiliates.

ISBN-13: 9781477829509
ISBN-10: 1477829504

Cover design by Kerrie Robertson

Library of Congress Control Number: 2014958169

Printed in the United States of America

1. MISTAKEN IDENTITY

"Samantha! Sam! Hey, wait up! Samantha Barnes! Wait!"

My footsteps quicken as I sigh, annoyed at the guy who is shouting behind me. It's amazing his voice has carried through the crowd on the street for as long as it has. It's also amazing he hasn't caught Samantha Barnes yet, whoever she is.

I have to assume it's one of two scenarios—either he's slow as molasses on a cold day or she's a gazelle and is way ahead of him.

"SAM!

"SAM!

"SAM, WAIT!"

Finally, I turn back to tell him he needs to run a lot faster or give up the chase, but the guy shouting is looking at me. "Sam, seriously, how fast do you walk?" He huffs and puffs like he might blow down the store next to me. He's slight, sort of a teaspoon of a man. He looks like he's going to take a knee or maybe just pass out altogether. His slim face is red and flushed.

I glance behind me, noticing no one else is stopped.

"I was running—for three blocks!" he gasps. He points and wheezes, "I knew—it was—you—whew! You walk—fast!" He has a slight overbite and spit on his bottom lip from the huffing and puffing. My nose wrinkles involuntarily at the heinous sight of the spit bubble.

I'm lost on whether or not he'll wipe it away or if I'll have to stare at it whilst he gets me mixed up with whomever he is looking for.

"You—walk so—fast." His breathing is still labored, and his face seems to be getting redder. For a small guy, he's awfully out of shape. After a moment, he runs his hands over his face, wiping away the sweat from his brow, and yet leaving behind the spit.

Lovely.

He does a huge sigh before speaking with the labored gasps. "I knew it was you when I saw you at Menchie's. How are you? It's been so long. Since what—second year, right?"

I shake my head, still mesmerized by the spit. Surely he feels it. Should I pull out a tissue and wipe it for him? How is it so bubbled and frothy?

He sighs. "It's me, Ronald Armstrong. We were at Berkeley together a few years ago." I cock an eyebrow, about to tell him he is mistaken, but he assumes it is an answer to his remark. "I suppose you're right, it wasn't a few years ago. Jesus, it was twelve years ago. That's right, you missed the reunion. I didn't go either. I saw your name on the list of people not attending."

I am drawing a huge blank. I never attended Berkeley, and I have never met him.

He smiles wide, flashing that overbite. "The year you left in the middle of the second semester, I heard you went FBI. You still with them?"

I nearly laugh, right in his frothy spit bubbler. "No." Whoever Sam is, she is clearly smarter than I ever was. I offer him a weak smile. "I'm really sorry, but I never went to Berkeley. I never went to college. You must have the wrong person."

His eyes narrow, and I can see the wheels turning, but he doesn't believe me. He relives every moment that in his mind we have spent together and then shakes his head. "No, I remember you. You sat in front of me. We weren't exactly friends, but I remember you. Is this an FBI thing?"

"Sorry. No."

"We always called you Sam, and you were really smart, sort of an activist, if I recall."

I shake my head again. "Jane. My name is Jane." My yogurt is melting, but I can't eat it while I stare at the white frothy spit bubble on his thin lower lip. I ponder the possibility that he will run after me if I just bolt and eat my yogurt in an alley.

He pauses a second as if processing the statement before he chuckles, rolling his eyes. "Oh shit. You're messing with me. Jesus, you almost had me too. You look so serious. Man, I forgot what a joker you were. That's crazy. Jane! Good one." He uses his hands to make movements like his head has exploded. He has thin fingers. They bother me.

He laughs, and something about him does seem familiar. But I think it's more that he has one of those faces—those rat faces that seem very similar. He points. "So how have you been?"

I give up and play along. "Good, and you?" I hope it will go faster and I can just get this over with.

"Good." He nods, finally wiping his lips on his sleeve and saving me from the horror of the white spit. "Great, really good. I got a resident position in France, actually. I'm heading there in a few weeks. It's just outside of Paris. They even have a residence for me so I can live for free while I finish my PhD. I'm so glad I switched my major. It means longer in school, but this opportunity is just such an affirmation that I made the right choice. Such a score."

He might as well be speaking German.

I nod along. "Wow, that's amazing." Is it? I don't know. I don't care. I don't give a shit. I just want to eat my frozen yogurt before it's no longer frozen.

He laughs. "Yeah. I feel pretty lucky. What are you doing?"

"I work in a shop." I point. "Just around the corner. I'm late, actually, from my coffee break. It was nice to see you—"

He smiles. "Ronald."

"Of course. Have a nice day and enjoy France."

"You want to get a coffee and catch up sometime?"

I shake my head. "I have to get back to work."

He looks like he might say something but he doesn't. He waves and watches me walking backward, desperate to escape him. His eyes bother me. Something about it all bothers me.

I turn and disappear into the crowd, taking the sneaky way back to work, and end up being really late from my break. The rest of the day sort of flies by. I don't even know where it goes, just that I look up and it's over. I close the shop and head home.

But Samantha Barnes never leaves my head. *Who is this doppelgänger I apparently have? And why in the gods did she attend Berkeley?* Unless, of course, she's actually an activist, then Berkeley makes perfect sense.

I round the corner home, lost in thought. Derek has the door open for me before I even stand a chance at turning the knob. "There she is, the most beautiful girl in the world." He smiles, but I scoff because between the two of us, it's more likely he's the most beautiful one. And a doctor to boot. Why he's with me is the mystery. He pulls me in, breathing an entire lungful before kissing the side of my face. "God, I love you."

I don't know how I got this lucky. I don't know why a magical man like him would ever have picked me.

Truth be told, I don't remember when we met.

I don't remember why it was me who got lucky with a man like him. That time is on the other side of my brain, the side I cannot reach.

He sweeps me into his arms, nearly crushing me, and murmurs, "Was it a great day?"

I nod against his soft cheek, staring at the open door to our house as a scent wafts out at me. "Did you make chicken Parm?"

"Of course. I always aim to please, milady." He pulls me back, offering one of those smiles I've seen make the girls at work melt. I don't melt, but I know if I were a normal girl I would. If any boy in the whole world could make me melt, it would be him. His eyes are dazzling green, with a hint of gray that only shows depending on his moods. It's the strangest color combination. His smile is sexy and lopsided because he has a larger incisor on the left than the right, making one side of his lips stick out a little. I like the fang-like tooth, though. It makes him look like a vampire in the right light. I have no idea why I find that sexy.

Clearly I was a freak before I lost my mind in the fog. He dips and kisses me again, pressing our faces and bodies up against one another.

"You made that just for me?" He hates chicken Parmesan, which is crazy. I love it. I don't think I love anything else, but I love it. It and the feel of my cat, Binx. He's soft and fluffy and mean. I adore his meanness the most.

Derek brushes a large and yet perfectly groomed hand through his dark-blond hair. "Baby, I've got an OR time. I have to go. Which is why I made your favorite dinner. So when I'm doing my surgery, I'll know you're thinking about me."

"I always think about you." The words are plain, not meant to be charming or schmoozed. I don't do that. I don't know how to be charming.

He kisses my lips again but this time so delicately that it makes my stomach growl for more than the dinner he's prepared. "I love you," he murmurs into my cheek before brushing past me, waving as he runs to the car.

Watching him head off makes me smile, even if I didn't get to tell him about my weird day or about my melted yogurt. My world and my news are never anything compared to the stuff he does. He saves lives, creates hope, and heals the sick. I wish I had gone to college and become something amazing like him.

He honks and blows me a kiss from the Mercedes. I wave back and head inside, excited for my meal. He always makes it extra saucy so that when I drag my garlic bread through it, the sauce soaks into the bread. He's a wizard, I swear.

I can't help but grin like an idiot when I see the table is set with a pink rose placed across my plate. They're my favorite.

Dinner is in the oven, making the entire house smell of his skill. He is an amazing chef.

He's amazing at everything.

One day I am going to wake up and realize this was all a dream, a wonderful dream but a dream nonetheless. There is no way he's real and mine.

I pull out the casserole dish and place it on the table. He's picked out the wine—he does that every time. I love the way he orders for me and picks the wine and makes everything work together to bring me the best.

He's a twelve, and I'm at best a seven. If you took my crappy job into consideration, I'm a five. His job makes him a fifteen or seventeen.

The cooking is like icing on the awesome cake.

He's tall, six foot two, and almost no body fat. He runs and lifts and eats low carb. He lives like he wants to live forever. His dark-blond hair is always styled nicely, but he doesn't look too groomed. He has that California glow, regardless of being from the East Coast.

He drinks weird infused waters and always takes his vitamins. It's annoying.

We are polar opposites. My dark hair and puffy lips make me look like I might be a touch ethnic, but I'm not. My father was English, and my mom was Scottish. I'm short, five four, and curvy. My body fat is probably near the low twenties, and when I run, I cramp up. I never run, I hate it. And by some small miracle, he doesn't care. He kisses every curve and loves every inch, and I never feel like I'm not enough. I know I'm not enough, but he would die if I told him I thought that. He loves with every ounce of himself whereas I don't know how to give any part of me. He doesn't even care that I don't know anything that has happened beyond three years ago. He reminds me who I am and what I like, and helps me find myself.

It's much more like dating a nun or a saint. Only he's sexy and likes giving oral sex too much to go in either of those directions. I do love that man, though. I love his heart and his way of giving me everything without my ever asking for a single thing.

I lean my face over the plate, closing my eyes and taking a deep breath. The first bite is incredible. The basil and Parmigiano-Reggiano swirl in my mouth, enhancing the slightly sweet marinara sauce against the perfectly crisp chicken. I am in food heaven.

When I finish, the name Samantha Barnes is still bouncing around in my head like a Ping-Pong ball. Drumming my fingers against the mahogany table, I push myself back and walk to the computer to Google her. The name comes up a hundred times on Facebook, LinkedIn, and MySpace. I click on "Images" instead of words, scrolling past all the different varieties of Samantha Barnes there are. There's a chef, a celebrity, a model, and a schoolteacher. The most intense has to be the bodybuilder Samantha Barnes—she's so ripped. I rub my food belly, gawking at how hardcore and rippling with muscle she is. I scroll down, stopping the moment I see the reason Ronald stopped me on the road. It's so shocking my eyes are torn from the bodybuilder chick.

I click on the black-and-white thumbnail photo of me as my jaw drops.

She can't be me—she grew up in Alabama, in a town I have never heard of. She went to Berkeley but it doesn't say graduated, and she died in some place called Fairhope. The resemblance is so uncanny I cannot believe I'm not looking at a picture of me with blonde hair.

The fact that an identical girl named Samantha Barnes exists is one crazy moment for me, but that's not the craziest part. For me, the most peculiar aspect of it is that she died six years ago in a fiery car crash. I was in a fiery crash three years ago. *How odd!*

I click on the newspaper article to read more.

Sunday night as the sun was setting on Fairhope, the owner of the Simple Pleasures Book Shop, Samantha Barnes, died in a car accident described by witnesses as horrific. Police Chief Langley speculated that her SUV was being driven too fast for the wet road conditions. He mentioned the car might have slid on a newer section of asphalt.

It took fire crews several hours to get the blaze under control as the flames incinerated the car and several trees nearby, including the large oak that the car struck.

The mayor of Fairhope had this to say: "It is a sad and tragic day. Sam was one of the upstanding citizens of our quiet town. She will be missed and always remembered fondly."

Barnes leaves behind a cat named Binx that her friends have adopted.

A cat named Binx?
A car accident?
A girl with my face and eyes?

I don't know what to say, and even if I did, my throat is tight with confusion. It's so parched it feels as if I haven't drank in a month. I click on the next link, finding comments from local towns-folk about the tragedy. Many people still sought answers as to who the other person in the car was. Some comments mention a man from another town. Reading it all makes me oddly uncomfortable, like I am bothered by the loss of a look-alike of me. The interviews with the townspeople make it seem as if she didn't have any family. She was single and died with a stranger who is still unidentified, even though it's six years later.

I Google her more, obsessed at the similarity in looks and life. I find a picture of her outside of a restaurant with several people. She looks uncomfortable. I know that face. I make it when people take *my* picture too.

I can't help but wonder if we are related, regardless of knowing my history. My parents died a year apart when I was eighteen and nineteen, hence the no college. Sam's parents must have been dead when her accident took place or they would have been interviewed or at least spoken of in the article. It's weird we were both alone. It's even weirder that we both had car accidents, though mine was only tragic to my brain. The rest of me has healed nicely. The name of the cat is creeping me out the most. I can't deny the odds are stacked way against us both picking a name as unusual as Binx. It's com-pletely unlikely.

It's strange. *Coincidental* is the word I want to use, because I don't believe I ever had a long-lost sister. But the name of the cat is too much to be coincidence. It doesn't add up.

I open our pictures on the computer, scrolling through them, looking for one that might be the right angle to match her picture. When I get one, I just sit and stare. It's uncanny.

Eventually, I have to turn the computer off, as my eyes feel like they have crossed from staring too long at the same pictures of her and me. The pictures prove her face and my face not only match, but blend—seamlessly. Even the slight lift of the right side of our mouths when we half smile is the same. Our eyebrows arch in the exact spot. The puffy lips have the same creases in them, and our eyes have the same laugh lines.

Completely confused and incapable of comprehending any of it, I curl up in the warm and fluffy bed that feels too big without the large man who's normally there. I need him to come home and tell me that I'm hallucinating.

It's no wonder the weird man on the street was so convinced. She and I are identical.

I don't know how long I have been asleep or how long Derek has been home, but when I wake it's still dark and he's kissing me softly along my neck. I moan and curl into him, smelling the soap and deodorant that makes up the scent of a doctor.

He wraps himself around me, pulling me into him like he never plans on letting me go.

It's a wonderful way to sleep, cocooned in a man who makes you feel like nothing matters beyond the two of you.

Not even an exact replica of you!

2. LOVE IN ALL THE WRONG PLACES

In the morning, not wanting to wake him as I sneak off to work, I write in my pale-pink lipstick on a napkin:

Missed you last night! See you later, xoxoxo!

It's something I do. It's my sad attempt at affection.

The morning flies by, and when it's time for lunch I hurry off to get a sandwich to eat in the back room. I like eating back here, I don't know why. The concrete room is uninviting, and yet I am completely at ease here.

The minute I come out from the back room, my Scottish boss, Angie, gives me a wink. "Ya had a visitor while ya was out!"

I stop, giving her a puzzled look. "What? Did Derek come here?"

"No, no. It weren't him. Like I'd tell ya if the doctor himself were here. I'd keep that one to meself. But there was a man asking for ya, but by a different name. Very strange."

My stomach drops a little. "By a different name?"

"Aye, he came right into the shop and demanded to see ya. Was up to no good, I could tell."

"To the store?" I shake my head, lost in the possibility that anyone would come to see me. "Here? To see me? Me specifically?"

"Well, ya, but he had a different name for ya. Quite the funny story, though." She laughs as she passes me the cleaning supplies so we can redress the mannequins in the front window and clean it. She wipes and natters on, regardless of the look I am certain is on my face. "He was tall, bloody tall, and he had an accent—Irish, he was. Never trust the Irish, if ya can even understand what the bloody hell they're saying to ya."

She's a fine one to talk—her accent is hilarious. She is Scottish and sort of prejudiced against everyone in Europe. She hasn't lived in Seattle long. Not long enough to decide if she likes the city or hates it. Apparently, she still hates the Irish, though. And the English. And Germans. And Polish people. She hates everyone, including us "bloody Yanks" who are always "bloody rude" to her and ripping her off. She kills me with all the things she hates and then loves in a bipolar sort of fashion.

She wrinkles her nose. "I mean, if he was even looking for ya at all. He seemed a touch confused." Her comment confuses me, but I have to assume it's friggin' Roland or Ronald or whatever the hell that guy's name was who was looking for Samantha. "He was Irish? You sure? Not a skinny American with an overbite?" I ask casually, making my fingers the teeth in the overbite, which actually makes no sense at all. I look like an idiot, with my fingers hanging over my lip.

"No." She pauses, giving my mimicking of the overbite a weird look. "I'm pretty sure I know a bloody leprechaun when I see one."

Oh God, please do not start with the racial slander again.

"What did he say? How did you know it was me he was looking for? Maybe it was just someone else." It's weird that two men have showed up in my life two days in a row, both looking for me with a different name. "You said it was a funny story, but that doesn't sound funny."

"Right! With his wee little accent, he said he was looking for a good time and needed the number of a girl who worked here in this very shop. She met him in a club downtown and promised him love in all the wrong places."

I groan, seeing now that she's dicking with me. She does this sometimes to mess with me. Of course, the day after I find out I have a dead identical twin, it isn't as funny as it normally would be. My heart is racing and I feel faint, but at least she's just being crazy and trying to get me going.

"Ya like that one, eh? Love in all the wrong places?" She winks.

I roll my eyes, trying to take deep breaths and get my heartbeat back to a comfortable range. "Ewwww, for starters. Not to mention, I don't club. And what does that even mean—love in all the wrong places? Is that like in an alley?"

She waggles her eyebrows at me. "It means—ya know—anal."

My jaw drops. "What the hell? Exit only, Angie. I don't know how you all like to do it, but for me that is exit only."

"It's a joke, ya wee prude." She tosses a handful of paper towels at me. "He never got your name right, so I dinna think he was looking for ya. I'm only teasing."

"What was the name?"

She stops laughing and gives me a funny look. "What?"

"The name of the girl he asked for."

"Samantha." She shrugs and carries on cleaning. "Blonde who worked here named Samantha Barnes."

I drop the window cleaner.

"What? Is that yer porno name? Yer making films with that handsome wee devil, aren't ya?"

I shake my head, trying to get a grip on my mind and the spinning room. "No." I'm not answering her. The *no* is a dramatic statement. I close my eyes for a moment. "What did he look like?"

"Tall, dark, hair, broad shoulders and chest, and blue eyes. He was quite good looking so I gave him my number. Told him if he could get rid of that bloody accent and talk like a gentleman, he could take me out, instead. The Irish always swear a lot."

That is not Ronald at all. Two men in two days is far more than alarming. I can hear the joke in her tone, but my heart is racing and my mouth is dry. I force a husky laugh from my lips and nod. "You should have made him stay here." Two Samanthas in two days? Two? *Is that possible?*

Not even mentioning the fact we named our cats the same fucking name. The concrete room is calling me back there, to my sanctuary.

She laughs, still not taking it as seriously as I am. "Yeah, well, he looked like he was busy. Had on a suit and tie and a briefcase, thank you very much. He was very official looking. Quite clean, considering where he's from. No tattoos or spiky hair." She makes a disgusted face.

The world feels like it's closing in around me, but I force myself to nod, swallowing hard. "You are so racist."

"It's not racism, it's common sense. Maybe he's from before . . . the accident, you know?"

I shudder but don't want her to see. "Yeah. Maybe I have a rich Irish husband somewhere looking for me." Oh God, what if I was somehow living a double life? Did I have a mean husband who wanted anal? Was I a stripper before I met Derek? No wonder I don't want to remember now. The only problem with that, though, is it isn't the story Derek has given me. Nothing is making any sense. How is it possible Derek doesn't even know I have a twin?

"What more could a girl like you ask for? I guess he could be from Scotland. That would make him better—only a wee bit, though."

I answer her with a look. She shakes her head, still chuckling and unaware of the crisis we are actually discussing. She glances at me sideways. "I'm only teasing ya! Derek is a fine man, nearly perfect. I mean, he is a Yank, after all, but he could be worse—he could be English. They're all tossers with bad teeth."

"You can't hate everyone, crazy." I laugh, desperate to not think about it all. "And maybe you should consider holding your Klan meetings elsewhere, psycho." I can't shake the uneasy feeling inside me at being mistaken for my twin, our having the cat, and the fact that she died the way I should have. I've seen the photos of my car after the wreck; I should have died.

"Your mind is a-wandering."

I nod. "It is. What were we talking about?"

"You having a rich mystery husband."

"I don't need a rich husband. I like my life." I narrow my gaze. "We were talking about you being racist."

"Pshh, hating the English is natural. No self-respecting Scotswoman would dare say otherwise."

I cock an eyebrow. "You dated an English guy three months ago. Henry, remember? He was sweet. You and Dennis had decided to take that break, and I made you date. You had fun."

"Did you see the teeth on that mug?" She makes the finger teeth like I did and then scoffs. "Jane, in all honesty your life is pretty good. You have a fun job with me, a good man, and a very sleek town house in the city. Really, what more could you ask for? Derek is the best, and he's a doctor. Who cares if you don't remember stripping and doing anal?" She nudges me, and I can see this is going to be the joke we share for the next year.

Jane and the anal . . .

A grimace crosses my face. "Dear God. Okay, moving on." I turn to finish wiping the windows. I want to continue thinking about Derek and my amazing life, but I can't. I can't help but watch every person who walks past our shop. The cool of the autumn breeze causes the passersby to keep their faces down, making it hard to see which one might match the stranger who came into the shop.

I don't have an answer for any of it, but I feel sick, like my guts are twisting with guilt for some reason.

Angie hums as we finish dressing the plastic ladies and gents in the window. She always hums when we work, and the song is always the same with her, something her mother had sung when she was a girl. It's her song.

I too have a song. I assume it's from when I was a girl, like Angie's. But for whatever reason, my song feels like a secret. Even Derek doesn't know about it. I have never shared it with him. I wanted to, but I changed my mind just as I opened my mouth to tell him.

I don't know why.

I can't explain my idiosyncrasies or my desire to be private in all things. I don't know the old me or why she was like that, but I am still her in so many ways. Muscle memory and habits are hard to break—I have proven that.

Except in the memory department.

I have one song and one ability that I clearly learned somewhere. That is all that is left in the great empty barrel my brain turned out to be.

A head of nothing but two small things.

A song with a strange high-pitched tone, like it's mocking, and tying cherry stems with my tongue.

Beyond, of course, the things you learn as a child. I can count, tie my shoes, run, climb, eat, and speak. I can play hide-and-seek, hopscotch, and cards.

Things I think are unique to me but not learned—like I can lick my nose and flutter my lashes like I'm having a seizure. I laugh when people get hurt, and I cry when animals do. I like purple and green. My dark hair complements both colors perfectly. My blue eyes are slightly different colored: one is light blue and the other dark blue. I always find horses in cloud formations, and I love the History Channel and the smell of my cat when he's played out on the deck during the rain. I hate running. I naturally always pick the most expensive item on display. I can't play any sports, but I'm flexible.

I can shoot houseflies with rubber bands, sharpshooter style, and I can paint.

But there is nothing else.

Most days I don't wish there was anything else. But every now and then I get an itch like I want to know something, and I hate it when I can't reach it, or the emotion I assume is attached to it.

Like how I met Derek.

How did it happen?

How did I feel?

What did he look like the first time I saw him?

Was he crossing a room when the lights hit, glinting off him?

Did he give me the half look, where he lifts his face only a bit and smiles?

It's my favorite look. I've never told him that, but it is. He glances up through his eyelashes and gives a sly grin. I always imagine some dirty thought is roaming his brain, but I know it's probably more saintly. He's imagining building houses in impoverished countries and saving orphans.

"Och, listen to me humming away again." Angie nods at me, interrupting my thoughts. "How does that weird song go again? I tried singing it to me mum, but I forgot how it went."

A smile creeps upon my lips. "It's not weird. No weirder than that one you're always singing."

She positions the mannequin in the window properly and makes the plastic woman's head nod. "Sing it."

"Me or her?"

She flashes me a shitty grin. "Don't be daft. If she could sing it, we would be rich. Like that movie, where the mannequin comes to life and dates that wanker."

"I don't remember that one." I laugh. "Besides, you never know. Maybe I *am* rich."

"And maybe I'm the long-lost granddaughter to the queen." She scoffs and wraps a purple scarf over the throat of the mannequin. The way she does it, the way the scarf wraps so tightly, makes me stop. My eyes lock on the pale skin of the plastic girl and the tightly wound purple scarf. I can't swallow—I swear I can feel the itchy fabric on my throat. I move my head a little, as if it will loosen the scarf for her.

"Crazy coma patient." Angie waves her hand in front of my face. "You're doing it again. Just sing."

My lips open like I am a trained seal. "Listen, listen to the wind and stone. Listen, listen to the sounds of old. Listen, listen as my hopes are drowned. Listen, listen to the sounds that bullets make of blood and bone. Where will you run today? How will you ever get away?"

And there it is, one small section of a morbid song that, as far as the rest of the world is concerned, doesn't exist.

Angie gives me a funny look. "Still makes no sense. You sure that's the way it goes?"

My eyes lift to meet hers, but I am still stuck in the odd fog the lyrics give me, so my mouth remains closed. I nod and walk away, clutching the window cleaner and wondering if anything will ever make sense.

She is the only person I have ever sung the song to. She caught me singing it when I was working. I remembered it ages ago, but I never told Derek. I sort of hate the way he's always pressing me about my memories. It makes me feel like I should clam up more, like I did with the guy calling me Sam.

The idea of being pressed to remember makes me feel funny. I'm certainly the only amnesia patient who fears that she should avoid her previous life. The possibility of being an anal-loving stripper isn't making me feel better about my past.

I wonder if I should even tell Derek about the men calling me Sam or the girl who looked exactly like me until she burned up, dying the way I nearly did.

Derek is so intense about the memories. He thinks I don't notice that he presses my memories on a schedule, like a bus route. Mondays he does it in the morning. Tuesdays he comes and gets me for lunch and drops hints about it. Wednesday he doesn't do it. Thursday it's at dinnertime. Friday it's after sex—we always have sex on Friday. Saturday and Sunday he likes to do it randomly. Every week is the same.

Not that it matters. I am Jane. I like being Jane. Jane Spears is an uncomplicated girl who works in a shop and dates a doctor. A girl could do a lot worse.

I stay a bit late to help close the shop. When we're done we walk home, carrying bags of clothes from Angie's closet. She went through it, weeding out the clothes that were a little too ambitious for her size.

She nods at me as our heels click along the cold cement. "You know, I need to try the six-month-coma diet. You don't know for sure how old you are, and you're still a size four. It's like winning the woman lottery. You could have a bunch of little bratty kids running about while you're here free as a bird. You know how many women would die to be able to say they don't know how old they are?"

"I know how old I am."

She scoffs. "You don't. You only know what Derek has told you. It could be a pack of lies. Hell, I'd tell everyone that it *is* a pack of lies and that you're twenty-five for the next decade."

Her words mean nothing to her. They're a joke. But they couldn't have come at a worse time. For me they are a possibility I have never actually considered.

Could it be that Derek is lying to me about who I am? It is possible, though why would he? Why would he tell me I am a certain age and that my parents are dead? Why would he tell me I hate running and I love chicken Parmesan?

We pass through some steam, and something about it is familiar. The clicking of the heels on the cold concrete, the steam coming up from the manhole, and the way the cold wind pushes against my face, like it doesn't want me to walk any farther—I have done this before.

At some point and in some place similar to here, I have walked in heels through steam and the resistant cold wind. It had to have been an important moment for me to feel the dread I do now.

To anyone else it would be a "whatever" moment. To me it is almost like remembering. It is muscle memory. My body recognizes the actions, not the story.

When we get to Angie's building I realize she is midway through a story I have not heard a word of. Her pretty dark eyes are watery and sad. "So I said no and handed him his keys, and he hasn't called or come back home. I think he is actually living with her, so soon."

I stare at her, ashamed. She is my friend and I have not listened to something very terrible she wanted to share.

She must think I'm stunned silent from the shock, and she nods. "I know, right?" A single tear slips from her eye. "I know. I can't believe my marriage is over, ten years. Ten fucking years, and what do I have to show for it? I moved here to this cold and dank hell for him." She points at the clothes in the bag. "I can't fit into any of the shit I like, and my cat is depressed 'cause he's gone. She looks at me like I've chased him off." I stand there like a moron until she sighs.

"The appropriate response is a hug, Jane." She knows she has to tell me things like that sometimes.

Without a single hesitation, I step forward, taking her trembling body in my arms. She cries into my shoulder. It doesn't feel like a natural thing for me. It feels forced, but for her I would force anything. She steps back, smiling. "You make all this stuff feel small, ya know that? You're like my own personal dose of perspective. I feel bad about something, and you make it small just being here."

"Please don't say that," I say, shaking my head. "It's not small. Your marriage is over. Loss of love, loss of limb, and loss of life are all equal tragedies." I don't know where the words come from, but they sound right.

She smiles. "So it's okay for me to be sad, even though you don't know where you were three years ago?"

"More than okay." I hug her again. The second time it feels more natural. We stand there in the cold wind, wrapped in each other for some time. I don't know how long. I lose track of it as I literally feel my body expand to welcome her as my attachment grows with every piece of herself she shares. She is the only person I truly feel that with.

My arms tighten around her. She taps my back. "I can't breathe. Easy there, Frankenbarbie."

I laugh, stepping back.

She cocks an eyebrow. "So strong for such a small girl."

"I guess." I wink. "With my luck, I was a farmer's daughter."

"Now that's some wishful thinking." She snorts. "I could go for a cowboy. Maybe you have a cute brother." She turns to go inside. "Night, Jane."

I wave and turn to walk toward my town house, with the words I spoke running through my mind.

"Loss of love, loss of limb, and loss of life are equal tragedies." Where have I heard it before? It has to be from somewhere. Probably the place that my weird song comes from, or the place where I learned to tie cherry stems with my tongue. *A seedy strip club . . .*

The man coming in asking for love in all the wrong places still plagues me, much more than Ronald does. Ronald is easily explained. He went to Berkeley with my doppelgänger—twin—or maybe even clone.

But the man asking for services I apparently offered in a club downtown seems fairly far-fetched. The only thing it ties to is the cherry stem. In all honesty, that is an odd thing to remember. I can easily see a stripper tying a cherry stem with her tongue as a parlor trick. Or maybe the cherry was part of the "love in all the wrong places." That thought makes me shudder. But two guys looking for the dead Samantha in two days, that is odd. No matter how you slice it, that is strange. Strange and exhausting.

I walk up the driveway of my house, feeling the weirdest desire to circle behind the block and come in through the alley. The whole thing has me discombobulated. I shake my head and walk up to the door. My feet hurt, and by the time I get in the front door I am spent and confused. I don't even know how to explain the entire situation to Derek, especially not without sounding like I think maybe he has lied to me. Which I don't. I don't think that—I fear it.

In some way I don't want to tell him any of it. I just want the day to end the way it always does, with Derek pouring me wine and making me dinner. He'll talk and tell me stories about things I don't remember but I can imagine. Sometimes we watch a movie before we fall into bed laughing and snuggling. There in the dark, he will kiss me and whisper that he loves me more than a single thing in the world. I will close my eyes and forget that the world is full of holes. If I'm lucky he will make me feel safe and make the whole Samantha thing just a case of mistaken identity.

I smile as I open the door to him whistling, a sound he always makes when he cooks. The noise of him raucously clanging the dishes and cooking is my safe haven. Instantly, I sigh as I close the door and lean against it. I like the simple things in this house. I depend on them. They are what make me happy and at peace.

Binx comes to the door, rubbing against my legs and purring immediately. I scoop him up, rubbing my nose back and forth in his thick black-and-white fur. He hates the over-loving but he'll tolerate a minute of it. When I place him back on his paws he gives me his version of indignant.

Derek and I don't have plans beyond the cat and the city. We don't talk about marriage or kids, ever. I like not needing anything but him and Binx. If anything beyond a stubborn and independent cat needed me, it wouldn't live. I know that.

I don't have anything to give except awkwardness and a confused stare. But not to Derek or Binx. No, to them I am enough, awkward or not.

The phone rings as I put my stuff down and slip my shoes off.

"Hello." Derek's voice makes me smile again. Everything about him puts me at ease. He creates a comfortable place inside me. His was the first face I saw and the only one I remember.

He sounds winded when he speaks. "I'm not coming in tonight. I came in last night. I'm not on call, it's my forty-eight off. Where's Don? Fine, but you have to give me three days off. Fine. Be there in an hour." He hangs up his phone, sighing.

I walk into the kitchen and wrap my arms around him. He's so big, it's hard to wrap around him completely. I don't melt into him the way he forces me to when we lay together in the dark, but I give it my best shot. "Hi."

"Hey, I thought I saw Binx running." He brings his arms back and hugs me. "I guess you just heard that, huh?"

"Yup."

He spins, tilting my chin up. "I won't be long, I swear."

I shrug. "It's okay. It's not like you're a shopgirl. You're out there saving lives and shit."

"Don't mock shopgirls, I happen to be crazy about one." He lowers his lips to mine, gently placing the softest graze before taking a deep inhale of my cheek. "See you in a couple of hours." He kisses again, and I nod into it. He turns, blowing me a smooch as he hurries out the door.

And again I eat dinner alone. I wish he were here so I could tell him about my messed-up day. I wish he could tell me that none of it is anything and truly I am just one of the lucky few who found the person in the world who looks like them.

At least he made pot roast and roasted potatoes with a huge salad. It's delicious with the wine he chose. It always is.

It's almost better that he left; I doubt I would have been very good company. My mind is replaying a thousand different things. I want to Google things like *love in all the wrong places* and *Irish guys who knew Samantha Barnes*. I want to Google a bunch of things that won't lead to any answers and will only make me click links until I'm reading about the Irish revolution. I've been down this road before. Google is a tricky bitch.

I go to bed, convincing myself that it doesn't matter. I am Jane, and Samantha and her crazy life are over. Yes, we were identical. Yes, we both had a terrible car accident. Yes, we named our cats the very same strange name.

But my life is on the other side of the country, and I lived through my tragedy.

3. MISTAKEN ME

The next day, work feels worse than it did the day before. My feeble attempt at not caring ended before breakfast, and my brain is racked with strange thoughts, making it feel like my worries have tripled. It's odd considering two men who have mistaken me for a girl named Sam are nothing more than two cases of mistaken identity.

I know I am not Samantha Barnes.

But it doesn't feel like nothing.

In the bathroom I sit on the toilet and Google on my iPhone for answers to questions that aren't clear.

There's one article I find about people who look alarmingly alike, but the pairs of supposed twins are just similar, as in you might assume they're related, not identical.

I Google her again, becoming obsessed with her name and face. I widen the photo on the phone, almost dropping it when I see the fine scar along her chin. It's my scar. It's identical.

My whole body starts to tremble as if the temperature has dropped twenty degrees in the concrete room.

I zoom in, narrowing my gaze and then holding the phone closer and farther away. No matter what I do, I can't stop seeing myself in the picture or seeing the scar that before I never even noticed.

Two girls, on opposite sides of the country, who are identical, including scars, both have a terrible car accident. One dies and one lives but remembers nothing. They name their cats the same thing?

It doesn't add up.

It's a bad science-fiction movie.

Jesus, I am a clone.

I remember nothing because three years ago I was cloned from Samantha or she was cloned from me or I am the clone of Samantha. Wait, I said that already. I'm losing my mind.

But honestly, it's the only answer.

I wipe, realizing my pee has actually dried on my body, and wash my hands. In the mirror my eyes get stuck on the scar. I don't know how I got it. I don't know how I got any of them. Some are bad, from the accident. The worst is the one on my back that looks like a hole. It's where something stabbed in from the car. The slice across my ribs where they had to do emergency surgery is pretty grim. The only one I actually kind of like is on my forearm where glass shards cut me.

I have scars everywhere and remember none of them. I have given each of them a limited amount of thought, as they are foreign to me, like my past. They are part of the unimportant. The things on the other side of the fog.

But the scar on my chin just got very important. I wish the picture were in color so I could see if her eyes match in color.

I hurry out front and nod toward the door. "I have to rush home tonight. You mind if I'm off an hour early?"

Angie shakes her head. "No, go on with ya. I have to do some chatting with my lawyer anyway, and it's a cold day. No one is going to be shopping today."

I wave and dart out the front door. I'm nearly running when I get to the house, bursting through the door huffing and puffing like the big bad wolf.

Derek comes into the foyer, puzzled but smiling the moment he sees me. "Hey, you're early." I nod, but the moment he sees my eyes he loses his grin. "What?"

I hold my phone out with the picture showing. "Samantha Barnes. Who is she?"

"Don't know. Who is she?"

"Her." I hold it up so he can see better. "She's Samantha."

"This is you?"

I shake my head. "That's not me. Look at the date on that."

His eyes flick to the phone and then me. "Wow, she really looks remarkably like you. Different hair, though. Different look in the eyes too."

"You don't know anything about this?"

I think I see him check for humor, but when he doesn't find any, he swallows his laughter. "What? Know about what? No? I don't know the right answer here. Do I know a random girl who looks like you and failed to mention it? Is that what you're asking?"

"I think I've been cloned or am a clone."

The mocking leaves his tone completely. "As far as I know you have never been cloned. It's still illegal, as per my understanding. I could be wrong. I have been before. You recall that time when I thought the movie had Ingrid Bergman and you said no, it was Katharine Hepburn?" His joking is lost in the things I can't comprehend. And my hands are trembling when he wraps his around mine and pulls me to him, kissing my head while shaking his. "I have seen this a dozen times in other places and other people—identical people who don't know each other. It almost always turns out that they're related distantly or something along those lines."

"She could be my twin."

"No. You didn't have a sister, and you weren't cloned. You're a girl from California, and your life was amazing until three years ago."

I lift my face, still totally mystified. "But she is identical. We even have the same scar."

He smiles wider. "Everyone has that scar." He lifts his chin, sticking it out. "See!" It's true—he has the exact same scar. I never noticed his before either. "What brought this on? Is there something going on in your head? Have you been having delusions? Have you been keeping things from me?"

I shake my head again, hating the worried look I have placed in his eyes. "Some guy—some guy named Roland or Ronald or something. He came up to me saying I went to Berkeley and asked me how I was and called me Sam. I told him I wasn't her, but he was insistent I was Samantha Barnes. He was sure I was her. So I Googled and found this."

"Have you ever met this man before?"

"No. I don't know him. He truly just knew Samantha Barnes."

He takes my phone and reads the article. "Well, it's sort of sad, isn't it then? She's dead. She died in an accident."

"I could have died in my car accident."

"Oh, Jane, stop." He chuckles, sighing and looking at her picture once more. "I'll give it to you, it's spooky, but trust me—you are not her and vice versa. You are Jane, my Jane."

"Her cat was named Binx."

He chuckles softly. "There were many black cats named Binx after that *Hocus Pocus* movie. It's weird, that's all. I guarantee you're somehow related." He pulls me in tighter again, wrapping me in him. That's when I melt. I close my eyes and wish I could forget the entire three days, all of it.

He makes it so it doesn't even matter that there is a second guy calling me Sam. He makes it so it doesn't matter about my past or my clone. He makes everything better.

We eat in peace and don't talk about it anymore. It isn't an awkward silence; it's just different. I can see that I have stressed him out with my talk of clones and other fantastical things. That's the problem with brain injuries—you have one lapse in sanity that any other person might have, and people think you are crazy because you actually have the injury to make it so.

When we climb into bed, he kisses me on the cheek and whispers, "Let it go, Jane. No matter what, even if your mother did give up a child and you did have a twin—"

I tilt my head back to him to ask why he would say that, but he silences my questions with a finger on my lips. "Let me finish. Let's say, for argument's sake, she did give a child up—your twin, even. Your mother is dead; your father is dead. You were an only child, and you have no family in the US. Your parents emigrated from England, so you are fairly alone in this world, apart from me and Binxy. Do you need someone else to grieve? Is adding a dead identical sister to the mystery a good idea? Will positive things come from turning this into something to focus on instead of being in the moment?"

I close my mouth. He's completely right. He lowers his face, replacing his finger on my mouth with his lips. The kiss is soft and sweet but it changes quickly, becoming something more.

His hands lower from cupping my face to my body, pulling me in and under him. I don't think of another thing, beyond the caressing and sucking that starts so delicately and builds into a passionate frenzy. The way he moves when he's inside me, rocking me gently, makes me want to gyrate faster, speeding things up.

But I don't.

He controls the movement; he makes love to me. He worships at the altar that is my body, touching everywhere, kissing every inch, and bringing me to such heights that I forget all about my brief lapse in sanity.

He finishes with several great thrusts, pushing into me with force and disparity. I love it when he finishes and loses his constant grip on control. It's momentary and beautiful. I always watch.

I am the luckiest unlucky girl alive.

I am alive, and that's what I need to focus on.

4. CRAZY CAT LADY

Everything feels more normal in the morning air. Of course he's gone, leaving only a dent in the pillow and a satisfied feeling in my soul, and other places, to prove he was ever here at all. I love it when we make love. It's always soft and gentle, and yet somehow thorough in a way that ticks all my boxes.

He knows the boxes better than I do, so he controls the movements and the love we make.

I get dressed, not showering like I normally would. I leave the smell of him to linger on my skin. I love the smell of his body rubbed against mine.

The walk to work feels like a new day. Everything feels fresh and clean, making the cold, dank air a comfort in some bizarre way.

Angie grins when she sees me. "Someone had her a naughty night. Look at the sexy mess ya are."

"Shut up."

She winks. "Just tell me he made you supper and picked the wine and held you so tightly you couldn't even breathe."

My cheeks flush but I nod, giving her the fantasy of my perfection.

"Ya lucky bitch." She sighs and leans across the massive wooden counter. "What I would give for a doctor like yours."

There is nothing to add. I am the luckiest girl in the world and we both know it.

A woman comes in the store as I'm going through the morning start on the register. She gives Angie and me a shy smile. "I'm looking for a dress for a party tonight."

Angie walks to her, leading her to the dresses for dinner parties and charming her with the Scottish accent.

It's amusing to watch her in action. She is smooth and funny, and suddenly you're wearing something you swear isn't you, and yet with her you're comfortable.

I know this shy woman's pain. The mail lady walks in, always in a hurry with a fast smile and faster hands. She drops it with a nod and a wave and is back out the front door. The silly and relaxed grin on my face departs when I see the newspaper.

Ronald Armstrong is dead. The police are looking for clues as to how it happened but don't mention how he died.

They don't mention his name, either. He is a man, a random man, who is dead. The picture is hazy and funny looking. It doesn't improve on his overbite or skinny face. But I would know him anywhere, unless he too has a clone out there who has died unfortunately. His jowls and skinny face might haunt me the remaining years of my life.

Ronald Armstrong is dead, and I don't know how I feel about it all. I feel detached, yet like I should be feeling something for the man I never knew.

Angie and the woman come to the counter, carrying a dress and a wrap. Her eyes dart to the newspaper, lighting up like she's heard the tale or recognized the story. "Grisly, isn't it? The news said he was found down in Denny Blaine Park. He was on the beach, stabbed a hundred times or something."

My stomach drops. "That's terrible." I walk to the far side of the room, pretending to sleeve the clothes so they look tidy. But inside I am panicking.

I don't even know why.

I didn't know the man.

The woman leaves, smiling and happy about her purchase, as Angie opens the door for the deliveryman bringing the boxes of new inventory for us to hang and display.

She and the driver of the delivery truck get on like old friends. But I ignore them, desperately trying to sort the emotions I don't understand or completely feel.

There is something buried beneath the layers of things I cannot find in my head and heart that bothers me dearly about the random death of a perfect stranger.

"Oh, look at this one, Jane. It's so you. Have a go with it." She holds up a dark-red dress made of a satin-like fabric. It's deep and intense. I don't fight her on it but walk mindlessly to the dress she's holding up and take it, sliding the soft fabric between my fingertips.

I carry it to the changing room like a zombie, peeling off my sweater and slacks. In the mirror there is a flash of something beyond my pale-pink underwear and bra. Something of a history is there, beyond the scars and the red lines. It's a road map I suddenly need—crave.

I run my hands down the scar on my ribs, savoring the knobby feel of the ropey scar. The stitch marks on the sides are faint, but when I touch them I see something, a face. It's a man I don't know, not at all. He's shaking his dark hair, touching the scars with his thick fingers, but I don't shy away from the touch. The image might as well be a movie I've seen once. It's hazy and lost in a mist I won't ever wade through, not completely.

I drag the dress on, robotically. Angie was right—it's perfect for me. My long dark hair shines in contrast to the deep crimson of the dress. My small breasts are pert and perky, giving me the respectable amount of cleavage a proper lady wears. The creamy pallor of my skin is the exact color needed to wear a dress like this one. Too tanned or dark and you would bring out the orange in the red. But I am ghostly white, so the red stands strong. My oddly colored blue eyes and long lashes seem black under the bright lights, as if my pupils are the only things in my eyes.

I would look pretty, beautiful actually, if I could get past the frightened expression on my face. But it's fixed there, stunned and stuck.

"Let us have a look. Ya can't go putting it on and not show."

A small grin cracks my face, lighting up my looks a bit. I step out from the changing room, spinning for Angie to see. She clasps her hands to her ruddy face. "Oh, now. Och. Ya look like that actress Julie Roberts in *Pretty Woman*. Ya recall the hooker movie? Ya have to know that one."

"Julia Roberts," I mutter, correcting her but not recalling the movie even if somehow the actress's name slips from my lips.

"That's right—Julia, of course it is. Such a pretty girl. Where's she got to these days? Ya never see her anymore in films. Must be aging something fierce and hiding away."

I chuckle. "I don't know." I don't even know how I got her name out of the mud that is my mind. I can't even recall her face or if she looks like me.

"Well, we will have to put that in the window, what with the Christmas parties starting soon. Ya should get this one for Derek's."

I nod blankly. "It's nearly Christmas party time again?"

"Don't get me started on how fast the days are going. I'm nearly single again and almost forty. It's depressing." She turns and stalks back to the front of the store, leaving me to wallow in the puddle of my emotions.

The remainder of the day involves high-pitch squealing from Angie as she unpacks the inventory as though she has never seen it before, regardless of the fact she went to the shows and picked all the dresses, and me pretending to work.

When I get home I Google *Samantha Barnes, Ronald Armstrong, and Berkeley*, almost desperate to come across a photo of them together. There are many of him but none of her. The images of him are tags from Facebook and other social media. Samantha has none. Her name tags several other people with the same name.

It drives me to Google the thing I have avoided since I got home. The death. The murder is all over the news.

The pictures show a white van, several police, a scene taped off near some bushes, and a body bag.

The sight of it makes me ill just as Derek comes in the door with food. He puts it down on the stove, grinning at me. "I got Indian."

I close the laptop and walk into the kitchen, trying desperately not to let the death of someone I didn't know make me crazy.

He pauses, seeing the look on my face, which he reads like a book regularly. "What?"

"The man who called me Samantha Barnes was murdered in a park."

He cocks an eyebrow. "What?"

"Ronald Armstrong—he was killed in the park. He's the murder victim on the news."

Derek leans on the counter, running his hands through his dark-blond hair. "Jane, what are you talking about?" His eyes fill with worry. I hate it when he looks at me that way.

"Remember, I told you how there was a case of mistaken identity with Samantha Barnes? The dead man is the one who mistook me for her. And now he's dead."

His eyes narrow. "Baby, he's dead, but it doesn't have a single thing to do with you. The correlation is probably between him and being at the park at night. Maybe he was into drugs. It was Denny Blaine Park, wasn't it? That's a dark park at night."

"I know. I didn't mean I caused it." I don't know why I said it that way. I don't know why Ronald has affected me the way he has.

Derek smiles wide. I can see mocking thoughts roaming his head just by the grin on his face. But he doesn't entertain them. He abandons the bags, walks to me, and scoops me up. My legs wrap around his waist as his hands cup my ass cheeks. When our lips meet, my eyes close and everything else is blocked out. I run my hands up his neck into his hair, gripping it.

Something comes over me.

He tries to carry me to the bed to pay homage at the temple, but I grab the door frame, swinging him toward the couch. I struggle from his arms, pushing him onto the couch when I touch the carpet. I lift my shirt off, yank my pants down and kick them across the room, and climb onto his lap. He looks confused but I ignore it.

My fingers savagely pull his shirt off, forcing him to work with me, and position his head to kiss along my neck. Abruptly, I sit up, admiring him. His perfection is overwhelming. He's sculpted and hard in every place a man ought to be. I slide my hands over him as I rain kisses down his chest and abs. When I go to kneel between his legs, my knees dropping to the carpet, his lips part. A devilish amount of power surges through me as I undo his jeans and drag them down. He inhales sharply, still confused, maybe.

When I take him in my mouth there is a familiarity to this that's frightening. I know I don't remember ever doing this in three years. He leads the way. He controls the tempo. He runs the dance floor.

But there is a strange sensation inside me that resembles a memory, and it's positive I have done this before.

I slide my hand up his shaft as I work my mouth down, massaging with my tongue. His hands grip the couch, desperate and disoriented in the pleasure and unexpectedness of his loss of control. I can tell when he's lost in the sucking and touching because he starts moving with me, grinding the way I do when he plays with me. Knowing I'm about to rock his world in another way, I suck one last time before sitting back.

He looks up, flashing an expression I have never seen. His beauty has become tragic and pained. He looks uncomfortable and angry, and all of it turns me on more.

I climb up his body, sitting back on his rigid cock. I'm soaked from sucking him off and being in charge, so while the entry is rushed it's still perfect. Even I gasp, tilting my head back as I slide down his shaft.

The frenzy of bliss and powerlessness hits him, bringing him to life in a frightening way. He leans forward, gripping my hips with vigor, and forcing me to ride him the way he wants.

I let him go for a few moments, enjoying the feel of his punishing thrusts, matched with my rotating hips.

Then I push him back, shaking my head. There's a look on my face that I don't know if I have ever made. The flame in my stare is lighting my whole body on fire. I continue to ride him the way my body wants, circling my hips and sliding up and down at the pace that's perfect for me. He fills me in a way I don't think he ever has. It's too much if I sit the wrong way, but the pain of it becomes pleasure somehow.

Everything builds quickly, becoming part of the too much as an orgasm rips through me. The room blurs as the waves of pleasure shake me to the core. A bead of sweat trickles down my cheek as I stop, realizing we have both finished.

The room is silent, apart from our ragged breaths.

The air is heady with the spent frustrations and lusty rage.

The confusion is thick in us both.

He looks wounded or angry still but in a satiated sort of way.

I can see that the anger is empty of power. I have sucked every last drop of that from him. He doesn't say a thing, just stands, lifting me with him. His cock slips from me as he walks to the bathroom, carrying me to the shower.

He wraps around me as the water comes down, cold at first. I barely feel it as he takes the brunt of it but then opens us both up to the water when it's hotter. He strokes me and holds me, like we have made love his way. But the depth of his emotion over the event feels deeper than normal.

He feels different.

He holds me tightly, as if trying to trap me there in that sensuality. But he can't. I've done something different, and I liked it.

I can feel the difference in me from it.

We fall asleep that night without talking about it. I don't know what to do about that.

In the night I stir, unsure of the date or the time or even my name. When I wake, my memory is always a little worse, as if being asleep is akin to the coma I once lingered in.

When I do wake fully, I realize a smell has found its way into my dream, disturbing my sleep. The rusty and grimy filth of the smell picks at me, poking until my eyes are open. I blink for several seconds to let the memories of the evening wash back in.

It's still dark in the room, and he's gone. His inhales and exhales aren't part of the sounds in the room. His warmth is missing from the bed.

The smell becomes more important than his being gone. It's not bleach and it's not urine, but it's sharp like both those smells.

I sit up, feeling glueyness on my hands and noticing the way they stick to the sheets. It takes a second for me to remember washing up after we had sex. So it can't be from that. I wrinkle my nose and climb from the bed.

When I switch on the light it takes a moment before I see it.

The scent of the rust, the sharpness of it that cuts into my sense of smell, is nothing compared to the sight of it covering me in the stark bathroom lights.

Panicking at the sight of blood covering my hands and face, I run the taps, certain I must have had a nosebleed in the night. I wash everything, pulling off my pajamas and washing my abdomen where the blood has made its way.

I saunter into the bedroom, muttering about nosebleeds, barefoot and naked, to strip the bed. When I switch on my light I notice blood at the door, on the floor.

Like Hansel and Gretel, I follow it into the hallway, dragging on Derek's huge robe as I go. There are several more drops and even a handprint on the wall. "Derek?" My hands are shaking when I reach the front door to our town house, but the trepidation and fear tickling around inside me are nothing compared to what I feel when I open the door to outside.

The handle on the other side is covered in blood. The front steps have several droplets that lead toward the grass, but I lose them there.

I was outside?

I was outside covered in blood?

Or was Derek hurt?

My feet won't move and my mouth is dry, but my heart isn't even racing. I think it might have stopped completely. I don't feel scared anymore. I feel something else. Something I don't recognize, so I can't catalogue it with my other emotions.

It had to be that Derek was hurt and he tried to wake me but I was so asleep that I didn't stir?

Did he go to the hospital?

What the hell is happening?

I grab the cleaner from under the sink and spray Lysol everywhere—the handle, the blood spots on the deck, the stairs, and even on the concrete.

My body reacts with such fervor and command I almost don't recognize myself. The response I have to the sight of the blood is not the one I would have expected. The mess is cleaned within minutes, and the cloth is in the sink. Something comes over me. It's an odd thing to do. I grab the lighter fluid from the junk drawer, rags from the cupboard, and the matches from under the sink. I douse the rags in lighter fluid before placing them in the barbeque and tossing a match.

There's a pile of billowing black smoke when I realize what I have done.

But I don't stop there. I bleach the sink and grab my clothes and bedsheets, still on autopilot, and drag them to the metal garbage can. I pull the garbage bags out and dump the clothes and sheets into the metal can. Swiftly, I get the bleach and dump it on the clothes and sheets, soaking them in the entire gallon jug of bleach. My eyes burn and my nose waters, but I don't stop. I stir the garbage can full of bleaching linens with my broom handle and then drag the can out into the street. I pour it down the sewer drain, pushing the linens back as the bleach drains into the sewage.

I know it's wrong but I don't stop myself. It's like I can't.

I drag the can back to the house and dump the bleached laundry into the washing machine and start the load on hot.

I finally have a grip on myself when I'm spraying the can and dumping it on the driveway.

I don't know what it means, or why I did it, but I have to assume being that efficient at getting rid of bloodstains has to be a bad sign.

First the aggressive sex and now this.

How odd.

I send several texts as I sit at the kitchen table awaiting Derek's arrival home. He doesn't answer me for an hour. It is the longest hour in my life. Well, in three years, anyway.

I can't imagine where he is or why, until he messages me that he got called in, and he's in the doorway a moment later. "Jane?" he calls out in the hallway.

"In here."

He comes in, still in his scrubs. "You okay?"

I shake my head, swallowing hard. I don't really know where to begin, so I start with a question. "Did you get injured and try to come and wake me up?"

"No. Why?"

My eyes don't leave the square pattern in the tiles on the floor when my lips part again. "I woke covered in blood, and it was everywhere."

"What?" He drops to his knees, looking me over. "Are you hurt? Was it a nosebleed?"

"I'm not hurt. That's the weird part. The blood trail led me outside, where my bloody handprint was on the knob. So it seems I came into the house and got into bed covered in blood."

He tilts my chin. His eyes are filled with something very bad, but I can't discern what it is. I know it's bad, I can see it, but he has never made this face before. Not in the three years I recall, anyway. "You don't remember anything?"

I shake my head.

"I don't see any blood."

"I cleaned it up, like forensically cleaned it up."

His eyes close and his brow knits. He is devastated. "I think it's best if we go away for a while, Jane."

I shiver with fear and the harshly suspenseful words. "What?"

"I have something to tell you. It's not going to be easy, and I know you're going to be very angry with me, but I need you to hear it all before you react." Derek opens his eyes and swallows, bracing himself, maybe.

"I don't want to know, whatever it is."

He chuckles like he's exhausted. "You always say that."

"What?"

He trails a finger along my arm, tickling. "This isn't the first time we've been in the situation we are now. This isn't the first time you've woken covered in blood or worse."

There is nothing I can say or want to say. I sit frozen and scared as he struggles with something until finally whatever it is wins or loses and he blurts out, "Your real name is Samantha Barnes."

My stomach drops into my bowels.

He winces. "We met seven years ago. You were beautiful and fun and sexy and crazy. You were an amazing girl, and I loved you from the moment we met. But after a few months I started to notice things—weird things." He gets up and pours a glass of water, leaving me with those sentences.

"You lied to me?"

He nods, drinking the entire glass in one go.

"Why?"

He turns, looking worse than before. "Because the weird things were you waking up covered in blood. It was a small town that you lived in, so when bodies started popping up, coinciding with your night walks, I knew you were the one doing it."

Hot tears drip down my cheeks as the words refuse to make sense in my addled brain. I shake my head, but I can see the tears in his eyes.

"I faked our death. We were dating. I was doing my practicum in a town about fifty miles away, so no one knew me. I burned us up, burning the car so hot it would seem like our bodies were incinerated, apart from a few bones of course."

"Who did you burn?" The question frightens me and I suspect the answer will more but I need it.

"The hospital where I worked. I got them from the morgue, they were going to be cremated anyway." He has to be lying. "There was nothing left but bone chunks and jewelry."

My trembling lips part. "Why would you do that?"

He wipes his face, staring at the wall, refusing to look in my eyes. "Because I loved you and I needed you, and I knew if you were killing things at night they would lock you up in a mental ward. I knew I could take care of you and help you keep it under control."

"Things? Not people?"

He shakes his head, sniffling and wiping his eyes. "You never got that far. It was animals, mostly wild animals. I followed you once. You were like a sleepwalker, but you were ravenous. You killed a cat, smearing the blood on yourself, and then walked home. It was bizarre. I tried to talk to you, but you didn't see or hear me. Classic sleepwalking."

I cover my face in shame, wanting to block it all out. There is no way. I would never hurt a single thing. I don't have it in me. I know that. I can feel it. Especially a cat. I have Binx.

Thinking of his name sends me into a panic, wondering if he is the thing I killed. I lift my head, but my panic is instantly deflated as I see him crashed on the couch. He's sleeping and fine.

I close my eyes, shaking my head and wishing I could shake the words away. Wishing I could take them from my memory.

He walks to me. I hear his footsteps on the tiles. He drops to his knees again, wrapping himself around me. "You're Jane now. You're different now." It isn't the response I expected.

"But I was her. I was a girl who had a life. I had a college education. I knew Ronald."

He rubs my back, kissing my head. "You did. You are a smart girl—no one is disputing that. But you have a disease, a sickness. So until there's a cure, I keep you safe as best as I can. No stress, no anger, no worry, no problems. You can't handle a job more intense than being a shopgirl. You need familiarity and calmness all the time. We will pack up and leave tomorrow, go on a little trip."

I freeze, stilled by the words he has spoken.

My blood is still and my heart stops, so every single aspect of this moment is untouched, untainted by anything else. I need to be able to remember everything.

My stomach falls somewhere inside me, making an instant ache.

I went to Berkeley? My name is Sam? I feel like throwing up. My past has finally caught up to me, and all along it was hiding here, with him. I trusted him, and he hid all of it from me. *Why would he keep lying all these years?*

I gag back the heave in my throat. I feel like I'm standing in the desert and he is across from me and the ground is breaking off, separating us. There is a massive split in the earth in front of me, and he is on the other side.

Tears splash down from my eyes as the reality of it all hits. Everything moves as if there is a delay, just like it did when I first opened my eyes from the coma. I see the memories I have of the last three years. They are all of him—him and Angie and me. Is Angie in on it? Does she know me? Did a man really come in looking for me, or was she trying to help me remember?

"What are you thinking?" His voice is panicked.

"That I don't know you or me. That the dead guy in the park knew me better than either of us."

"Don't say that." He lifts my hands, kissing them. "I love you. I just wanted you to have a chance to start over."

I lift my head. "You almost killed me with the car accident on purpose?" I open his robe I'm wearing, revealing my scars and naked body. "You did this to me to protect me?"

He shakes his head. "You really had a car accident. You really did almost die."

I don't know what to say or do or think. I don't know what is true. Killing cats sounds pretty far-fetched to me. It doesn't ring true inside me. What if he's lying about that just like he's lied about everything else?

His eyes and the look on his face are killing me, but I can't get past it all. It's too much.

He walks to the bathroom, not closing the door all the way. I don't know why that bothers me but it does. He always closes it. Is he in there watching me? Or am I becoming paranoid?

Something inside me, an animalistic instinct, perhaps, takes over. I stand, without thinking, and pull on my dirty clothes from the floor, a habit he hates but tolerates. *How many of those are there? How many habits do I have that he just looks past? How much of this is real love, and how much is lying to protect us?*

When I get into the hallway, I place my cell phone on the desk at the front door. I don't want to talk to him. Not yet. I need to sort through the things he's said and the possibilities in every statement he made.

I back up to the door, snagging my Chucks from the shoe rack on my way out, and slowly close the door.

I don't know what to do or where to go or why.

All I know is that when I start to walk toward the backyard, my body goes into something I assume is survival mode. It's no longer animalistic but more as if I already know how to do it.

When I get past the stairwell on the side of the building behind us, I'm sheltered from the view of the house. I pull on my Chucks and run between the buildings to the alley at the end of the road. It feels colder, and I feel more alone than I think I ever have.

I turn toward Angie's place, but my earlier thought dawns on me that she might be involved. And even if she's not, he will likely look there first when he realizes I have left. I turn around and walk toward the only other place I can think of—the bus station.

I pay for the longest ride I have cash for, and sit in the warmth. My brain gets stuck on his smile, repeating it over and over. Without him as my safe place I have nothing, almost literally nothing. I can feel Jane dying off inside me, but Sam is still a distant blurry image. I don't know how to be her. I don't want to be her.

There's a chance I am now neither of them. I am lost.

5. AGENT BARNES

His hands run up the insides of my pants, trailing across my inner thighs with tickles and feather-light touches.

In my dream, I'm lying back on the bed and Derek's telling me how beautiful I am. I laugh and make a joke about him wanting to get into my pants. His fingers brush across my groin just as I'm startled awake to the vile breath of a stranger groping between my legs.

My hand flies out, choking him. My other hand grabs his fingers from between my legs. I snap his fingers back, breaking bone and joints. He cries out, but it's hushed from the hand around his throat. I squeeze harder with my fingers, attempting to break the windpipe. I know that is my goal.

It scares me. I let go and kick him into the seat across from me.

"Fucking bitch!" he chokes out, cradling his dirty fingers.

Another man glances over at me from a few rows up. He gives us each a confused look. The pervert ignores the man and me, muttering obscenities and clutching his broken hand to his raggedly dressed chest.

I get up, walking quickly to the front of the bus. The seats up there are empty. I don't know how long I've been riding, but it's daylight again. I don't even know where I am. I don't see the city anymore, so I get off at the next stop. All I know is I'm starving.

I walk down the stairs to the cold cement and then down the street that's lined with buildings, cars, and houses. It's not the kind of stop a person like me wants to take. It's residential but not the sort of residential I'm used to. It's dirty and seedy. I walk along the sidewalk, glancing at the cars lining the road. My fingers itch when I glimpse the cars, as if I could take one of them.

It's not as comforting as I would have imagined, the possibility I might be able to steal cars.

The streets are nearly empty here; not a single pedestrian walks by me. I look over at the houses I pass, getting an even fouler idea. I need to sleep, shower, eat, and use the washroom. I need to do the things I should have been able to do at my house. I feel like Goldilocks.

Wishing I had my phone, I climb the steps of the next house I see with no car out front, and knock. No one comes.

I knock again, but there isn't movement in the house, so I walk around to the rear, slipping into the backyard. It's small and neat. I rub my hands together as I try the basement door. It opens. I stand there, watching my breath play with the cold air, and try to decide if this is the right choice.

I push the door open and call into the darkness of the strange basement. "Hello?"

There is no answer from the shadows, so I step inside, smelling something that makes me wrinkle my nose. It's musty and overwhelming. It's the opposite of our house.

I close the door and lock it behind me. It's the least I can do for the owners who have left their home unlocked for strangers like me to invade.

The basement is silent. There is no movement in the house, no water or footsteps or voices or heat. It's as cold inside as it is outside.

The back room is icy and dark. The only light comes from the window in the basement door. I stay there with my back pressed against the window.

If my feet go any farther I am breaking the law, badly, but my stomach is aching and I need to call Angie. Desperate to be warm and to speak to someone who will help me, I push myself off the door and force my feet to venture into the strange house.

The basement is old and dingy. It reminds me of something but I can't recall what.

Behind the misery, lies, and everything else, I miss Derek. I miss our home and the warmth we make there. In a spinning world of chaos he is the only constant thing I have to keep my eyes on, to keep me from falling. Now I don't know if I have him, and I feel like I might plummet any second.

I climb the carpeted stairs and realize the smell that is bothering me is smoke. It's old smoke. It worsens as I reach the top step of the upstairs floor.

A song plays in my mind, as if I am watching a movie the moment the smoke triggers a memory.

I remember a car ride and a lady singing a song on the radio. The Rolling Stones. It was the Rolling Stones. I don't know who she is, but she sings and reaches into the back to stroke my hair. Her face is fuzzy, like my mind. She tells me to stay low—the smoke will bother me less if I sit on the floor. I curl up and close my eyes again, and she sings softly. I can see the light through my eyelids.

The flash is there one minute and instantly gone the next. I make a conscious decision to make that a memory. My first real memory of before. I am strong enough to let the memories in and deal with what I find. I have to be. Besides, if I remember her I'm not alone. Maybe she is the mother I don't recall.

I walk into a living room and then a kitchen. Everything is older, not like our house. It's dull, like their life started in a small house and they will die in a small house and they will never matter beyond the block they live on.

I don't know why but that feels like a life not worth living.

My eyes take a second to adjust to the dull house. I am so lost in thought I forget why I'm here. Then I see the old phone in the corner. It looks like the one I saw in the picture books from my memory testing. I have never seen one except in the picture book. I brush my fingers against the smooth beige plastic of it, almost like I am unsure of how to use it. I press too hard on the top, and the handle falls off. I step back as it clangs, and I hear the dial tone.

Looking around, hoping no one has seen me come in, I pick up the handle and listen to the side with the dial tone. There are buttons to push like any other phone. I dial the shop and hope she answers.

"Lenora's Boutique, Angie speaking."

I sigh. "Angie." My voice is a whisper.

Hers drops too. "Where are ya? Derek's freaking out. He came to my house last night in the middle of the night, looking for ya, but I dinna know where ya got to. He said he has the cops looking for ya. Are ya all right? Did ya get in a fight?"

I shake my head. "I don't know what's wrong with me. I just need to figure some things out. Can I stay with you?"

She is silent for a moment.

"Just for a bit? I need to work out a couple of things."

She sighs into the phone. "I think ya should go with Derek, Jane. He seems worried about your memory again. He said ya seemed like ya were having a bit of trouble. Maybe being with a doctor is a good idea."

I'm racking my brain to figure out how to make her see how odd all of this is, but I can't. Not without explaining the cat killing and all the other horrors of my past. And especially not if her brain works the same way mine does. I already wonder if I killed Ronald or was responsible for his death in some way. If subconsciously I knew I was Sam and went to him and killed him. If Derek found me wandering and cleaned me up, and that's why I felt so weird about Ronald being dead.

My brain seems to think I am up to no good.

I blurt out the thing I have wanted to tell her since he said it. "My real name is Samantha Barnes. Derek just told me that—my real name isn't Jane. He lied to me and told me my name was Jane when I woke from the coma three years ago."

Finally, after several tense seconds she talks, again in a hushed tone, "He said your name *is* Samantha? Like the guy who came back today did? The Irish guy who demanded to know where ya were?"

"He came back?"

"Aye, this morning. He just left a few moments ago." She sounds funny. Her accent is thicker than normal.

"Did you tell Derek?"

"Och, no. The man seemed touched. He said ya were in danger and he needed to save ya. He said to tell ya they found ya and not to be scared of him. Course with Derek lying, now I'm not sure. I mean, what if ya are in danger?"

I shake instantly, like my body understands the threat. "What does that even mean? How does he know me?" Oh God, he could be the police. He could know I killed things—people. *What if I did? What if I did kill someone?*

"I don't know, Jane. I do know Derek has been here three times this morning. He keeps coming and asking if you've called. He looks like a wreck. What's his reason for lying? I don't understand."

"Me either." Emotions and ideas are both lost to me. I don't budge. I stand there in the dull kitchen, hating the stale air and life-lessness of the house I am in. I can't reach the way I feel or what I should do. So I ask her, "Now that you know he was lying to me, do you think I should come there?"

She sighs. "I don't know. Why was he lying to you?"

"I don't know." I can't tell her about the killings.

"Well, I agree it's all quite weird. The man who came in here— he was off a wee bit, but not like he wanted to hurt anyone or lie about who they are. He seemed desperate. Where are you?"

I look around the room, shaking my head. "I don't know." It's the truth. I don't know.

"Have you thought about going to the police? I might have done that first, not to sound smug or anything."

I wince, wondering why my instincts never took me to the police. "No."

"Just come here and talk to Derek here. That's what I would do. If he doesn't answer the questions you want him to or tell the truth, then you come home with me. No one can force you to do anything. You are your own woman."

Home. It's a nice thought, but inside my stomach there is a storm. My body is screaming at me suddenly. My hand drops the phone into the cradle as my body turns and runs from the house, long before my mind has a clue as to what is up. My brain is still wondering why I didn't use the bathroom or eat or shower or even lock the door. Instead, I run from the front door and across the road, down a block, and turn up another road. Glancing all around me, I duck into an alley and sit between two garbage cans with my legs tucked into me, holding them tightly and hugging myself as I lean into the fence behind me. The chain link makes a noise like someone is shaking it. Until I realize it's me trembling, and sit still.

The whole world stops for me when I hear a siren and then another. As if this has been the plan all along, I lift the lid off the can next to me and hold it over my head, like I too am a trash can. My eyes dart up to look at the lid, and I wonder if I'm psychic or a psycho. It doesn't feel like either, oddly enough.

It feels like I've run before.

Everything thus far has been a muscle memory. Everything has been as if I practiced it.

The crunch of footsteps in the alley gets my attention, but I don't move, just sit there between the large metal cans and wait.

Until I hear voices from the house in front of me: "She's had a massive heart attack. We need the police car out front when we head for the hospital, clearing the way." I close my eyes, listening to the voices. The sirens are not for me. They aren't coming to take me away for whatever shit I've done that I don't know about.

I sit there, not moving, and wait even though I am lost, tired, and scared. My own actions terrify me.

The footsteps crunching along the alley, to the right again, startle me. My heart starts to pound louder as they draw nearer. One man walks along the alley until his feet are directly in front of me. His boots look like he's a construction worker or something akin to one. He plucks the lid from my hands and tosses it to the side. "Miss?" I don't look up, struggling with the terrible feeling inside me. He drops to his knees. "Are you okay?" He's an older gentleman. He has a sweet smile and genuine concern on his face.

I shake my head. "Who are you?"

He gives me a funny look. "Stan. I live just over there. I wanted to go check out what the ruckus is. Are you all right?"

I shake my head again. "I hardly know."

He lowers his gaze to mine. "Those are cops over there. Wanna go see one and see if maybe they can take you somewhere warmer than this alley?" He offers me his hand.

I place my hand in his and nod. "Okay." I might actually be crazy and be a danger to myself. I did hurt that man on the bus, and I did wake covered in blood.

Maybe there is a reason I don't remember anything.

Against the animalistic urges inside me, I let him pull me down the road to the place where the police and ambulance drivers are.

The ambulance and half of the cops leave in a mad rush of sirens and lights.

Stan pulls me to a cop who is next to his car. He nods back at me. "Hey, I think this girl is strung out. I found her in the alley with a trash-can lid on her head."

The cop gives me a worried look as he tilts my face up. "You okay?"

"I don't know. I'm not strung out. I need to find my friend. She's in Seattle."

He sighs and nods at his car. "That's a long ways from here. Just get in the back and I'll give you a ride to the hospital in Seattle. I'm headed there anyway."

I almost argue but then I think about it. "Okay." A hospital sounds like a good idea. What am I running from? A doctor who loves me and wants to help me and protect me? Derek's story has to have a valid reason. There must be a reason for it all. No one protects someone the way he does me unless there is something they need protecting from. The lengths he's gone to speak of the love he has for me, more than the lies he has told can speak against it.

Either way, there is no way I am going to get anywhere without some answers, and I am not getting them by running away. All my answers are with Derek.

I climb into the back of the cop car, something that feels abhorrently wrong to me. My skin crawls and my mouth goes dry as I touch the vinyl seats. The man from the alley waves. "Feel better."

I nod and look down at the floor. When they close the door I have the strangest sensation, like being trapped. My mind is attempting to reason with me, but my body is panicking. Its instincts are not keen on the police.

It's weird.

6. A MAGIC COCK ON A MADMAN

Convincing the cop to bring me to the police station downtown was easy once I had him persuaded I wasn't strung out. But clearing my name in the system is making me nervous. The office I'm sitting in is filled with the scent of coffee and old shredded paper. I don't remember where I smelled shredded paper before, but I know the smell.

A man walks in, closing the door and leaning against it as if he's trapping me in there. He makes me uncomfortable instantly, making my stomach hard as a rock.

"Samantha?" His voice makes my skin crawl, but the fact he knows my real name is unbelievable.

"Jane Spears." I don't know why I lie, but it seems like the smarter move.

He chuckles, and I realize by the way he said my name that he is the Irishman. He is the man searching for me. He shakes his head, cocking it to the side with a grin that makes my stomach twist in knots. "What in the fucking hell are ya doing in Seattle, ya crazy bitch?"

I pull back, stunned and unsure of what to say.

"I've been searching high and fucking low for ya. I knew ya weren't dead. I knew ya just went deep with him."

I shudder from the cool in the room. I didn't notice it before, but I'm suddenly freezing.

"Did ya miss me? 'Cause I missed you." He cracks a bigger grin and takes a step closer but stops when he sees I'm trembling. "It's real then? The memory? It's not an act?"

I shake my head slowly, completely scared.

He moves cautiously with purpose to the desk, picking up a file and sliding it across the table to me. He nods at it. "Sam, you were my partner for five years. We were undercover together at Berkeley for two. We were undercover in Ireland for a year. We worked the assassinations of seven men and one woman. It's what led us to this case." He chuckles again as he takes small steps to the desk and sits slowly. Everything he does is purposeful and planned, like a tiger walking in a cage, always watching you.

I lift a hand, dragging open the file.

Everything crashes inside me. My emotions hit a wall of sorts, but break through. Hot tears flood my face. They try to blind me and block out the truth, but every page is another answer to a question I never thought to ask until recently.

I am thirty-two years old. I work for the American government in something that's blacked out on the files, so it must be intense if they won't even tell me about me.

My mother's name was Sheila. She died in a car accident when I was two. My father was an abusive drunk. His name was Leroy Anderson. I was abducted as a small child, taken by my aunt Pat, and raised as her daughter. Barnes is my aunt's name. She's still alive, living in North Carolina. The file says she saved me. She abducted me to save me from my father.

I have no sisters or brothers.

There are pictures of a cat, a black-and-white cat.

The tears try to block it all out, so I get blurry images of a history—schools, houses, and people that just can't be real.

It's all about me.

Me as a blonde, a redhead, a brunette. I am thin in every shot, much thinner than now.

"Aye, look how skinny ya were."

I lift my snotty face, crying harder.

He laughs at me, completely at me, as if we have a comfort level that can support that level of mockery. He hands me a tissue. "You look better like this. More real. You were always a bit of a Barbie doll before. So thin and pert. Ya look like a regular girl now."

I sniffle. "I don't believe this, any of it. I'm Jane Spears, and I want a lawyer. You're trying to make me do something I don't want to do. I need to go home. I demand to be released." Panic fills me as the walls creep in closer and closer.

"You don't know you're Sam, and it's gonna take some time to get you back on track. Just look at the evidence." He nods. "I would imagine you have spent a long time being lied to. How long since you lost your memory?"

Before I answer, I blow my nose and wipe my face. Trying desperately to get some sort of control over my emotions, I shake my head with my eyes closed. It's like being in Oz or *The Twilight Zone*. But when I open my eyes again, he's still here and I'm still some secret agent of sorts with a dead mother, an abusive father, and an aunt who might have actually saved my life.

"Answer the questions and you can go home."

"Three years. I was in an accident and got amnesia."

His eyes narrow in disbelief. "Were you hurt badly?"

I shrug. "I have hordes of scars. Derek said it was bad."

He scowls. "Who? You aren't with Dash anymore? Did you kill him? Fuck, he didn't get away, did he?"

My brow knits. "You have to ask questions I might understand."

He reaches for me slowly, stopping at the file to flip pages. He comes to a shot of a man who could be Derek, maybe, and thumps his finger down hard. "Dash, Benjamin Dash. Is he dead or alive?"

I swallow hard, worried about exactly what kind of trouble Derek is in. My instinct is to protect him. "I don't know this man."

He winces, wrinkling his nose. "Of course ya do. He's a skeezy fucker." He says it like *focker* and snorts. I have never seen a human being react that way to Derek. He's a god among men. "What were your injuries in the accident?"

"I have scars on my ribs, back, and my arm. My head has a small one under my hair."

"You've always had those scars. They're old as sin. I don't think you were in a car accident. I think he did something to your mind. Fucked with it. Feel like protecting him now? The old you was hard as nails and woulda killed him in a heartbeat. He's made you soft." He snorts and grabs a picture from the bunch of the blonde girl who is identical to me, in a bikini. The scars are the same. I had them before. They're not from the accident. His words cut through me, making new scars.

No accident is ringing in my head like Quasimodo is in there himself, pulling on the rope. After a second I nod. "His name is Derek, not Dash. He's a good man."

"A good liar, ya mean." He sighs, licks his lips, and slaps the picture. "What can you tell us? What have you gotten on him in the last six years?"

Every time he mentions how long it's been, he looks like he might hug me. I move my chair a little, backing away from him. I don't know what to say about the scars so I focus on Derek. "Nothing. He's a surgeon and a humanitarian and a good cook."

He bites his lip, furrowing his dark brow. "Right, and he's got a magic cock. How about the assassinations with their serial-killer tactics used? He doesn't assassinate like a normal cleaner would. Who does he work for? Why always political and royalty with him? Why not the average random, like normal serial killers?"

"He works at the hospital. I don't know." Tears build back up in my eyes again.

He slumps back in the chair, groaning. "Jesus, Mary, and Joseph, what the bleeding hell did he do to you? Ya baking cakes now for him, or what?"

"Who are you?"

He cocks an eyebrow, pausing as if he doesn't understand the question, before bursting into a fit of laughter. His dark-blue eyes narrow with the laugh, squinting with tears of joy. He's tall and broad, just like Angie said he was. He's handsome and chiseled—that's the word I would use for him: *chiseled*. His dark hair and tanned skin make him a perfect tall, dark, and handsome. It's too bad he cusses so much, just like Angie said he would. I almost want to record him so I can show her she was right. If I wasn't on the verge of losing my mind and committing myself into a center, I would actually do it.

He slaps the desk once more, wiping his face. "Rory Guthrie. I can't believe I never introduced myself." He reaches over, flipping to the section in the file about him and me. There are dozens of photos of us together. I blush when I see us kissing.

"Well, we had to be a couple, but we kept it professional."

There is a photo of us young and in Berkeley sweaters. Mine is gray and his, black. We look like typical college nerds. His hair is longer and fluffy and he has glasses, but it's like Superman and Clark; you can't hide his type of beautiful with some nerdy shit.

Seeing the pictures makes my heart flutter in the wrong sort of way. He instantly makes me uncomfortable. The smell of his cologne or aftershave fills the air.

"What do you want?" I ask.

"For you to finish the job you started."

I glance up at him, completely lost. "What job?"

"Bring in Dash." My eyes clearly answer the request, because Rory laughs. "You have to, or they're going to consider you rogue. You know what the charges for treason look like?"

My insides twist. "How can I? I don't know anything, and he's done nothing wrong. He's a good person; this is a mistake."

"You're still alive after six years. He clearly feels something for you or he would have killed you. He must know what you are."

I shake my head. "What am I? I work in shops. I'm lucky to have him. I'm the one you want. At night I sleepwalk and murder animals."

He cocks an eyebrow. "You're a fucking vegetarian! Stop the act."

I shudder. "No. I'm not."

"Yeah, ya are. Ya been one since you were five years old. Your dad was killing a pig in the barn. It was making all kinds of fuss. He was cocking it up 'cause he was drunk off his ass and you woke up, caught him, and freaked out. He fucking cooked the pig and made you eat it. You decided from then on, no more animals."

My throat turns sour. "You have to be wrong. I eat meat."

He sighs. "Well, I guess being with nutty old Dash has cured you of one thing. Thank God for that."

I push the images away, pretending the last ten seconds never occurred. "It doesn't matter. I woke with blood all over me. He told me I kill animals in my sleep."

He scoffs. "He rubbed you down with blood and lied to you. He's a sociopath. He's going to play with you, Sam. Get used to it."

"Jane. If that's the case, you can't expect me to go back there and pretend everything is normal."

"Your name is Sam." Rory nods. "And yes, I do. I expect ya to do your job. I won't go to the superiors yet. I'll give you a week to figure this all out. But the minute they find out you have amnesia, they're gonna haul you in for testing. No one wants CIA testing of any sort." He nods at the file folder. "Read it, memorize it, and get the fuck back home." He winks, and I think I might actually hate him a little. "Also, what's your cell phone number, so I can rig your line?"

I write the number down. I think I would do anything to go home at this point.

He flashes me the grin that makes my stomach ache. "Dial 911 from your phone to get me anytime of the day. If he leaves at night, you follow, and call me." He takes something from his pocket and slides it across the table to me. "Put this on the car if ya get a chance, so we can track it." It's a small metal magnet. It makes me feel instantly guilty but I pocket it anyway. "He's not a good man, Jane. He's a killer and a dangerous one at that. He's erased your memory and made you his simpering bitch. I need you to think about that. I need you to want revenge for it as badly as I do."

I want to argue, or at the very least, be offended by the "simpering bitch" comment, but I have run out of ammo. The evidence makes Derek look guilty. If he is, I will need all the help I can get, and if he isn't, I'll need to clear his name.

Rory leaves the room, so I spend the next four hours memorizing the contents of the file and praying this is somehow still a case of mistaken identity.

The information feels like too much, but my brain seems to come alive under the circumstances. There's a sickening thrill for the first few hours of reading, as if my brain thrives on the danger and adventure of it all. Finally, exhausted and unable to read another thing, I sigh and slip the file folder into the shredding machine and turn it on. I don't even know why I do that; it just feels like the right choice. I walk to the front counter. "Is he still here?"

The lady at the desk gives me a completely blank stare. "Who?"

"The Irishman I was with—Rory. Tall, dark hair, and quite handsome, but crass."

Her eyebrows knit. "I didn't see anyone like that."

"Of course not," I mutter and leave the police station.

On the way home my brain runs everything off like it's following a list of things to decipher.

Benjamin Dash is a genius. He's smarter than I am. He's a doctor. He's a psychopath? That one doesn't feel so real. The people who want me to bring him in suspect he's murdered dozens of people using freakishly devious ways to kill them. He's a master at making it look like an accident. That I could actually see—he's intelligent in a way that awes me regularly.

And then there's the fact he's in love with me.

But according to them, not me the way I was, me the way I am now. He likes me broken and needy. He made me needy on purpose. He made me soft and took away everything I was. I don't know how to feel about that, if it's true.

And even if it is, it's not like he took much away in reality. Looking back at the file I realize I wasn't much better off. I was stronger, more independent, and braver. But I was alone, working all the time. I was single. In every one of those pictures I looked sad or hard. I don't recognize that girl. She's sad and distant, and I don't feel that way anymore. So maybe he saved me from myself?

In all honesty I feel like I will wake any second and it will all be a bad dream caused by watching late-night TV again.

I feel sick that Derek has lied to me, but I see why, in a sick and twisted sort of way. I was lying first. I am still lying; we just didn't know it.

I ride the bus home with my last couple of dollars. I'm cold and hungry and exhausted. I can't kid myself—the moment I see the house, I'm elated. I know he's in there, cooking or waiting for me. I know he's worried and misses me. And I miss him. I miss who we were yesterday.

I don't even make the driveway and I see the handle on the door turning. Quickly, I slip my hand into my pocket, pulling out the magnet, and as I walk past the car I attach it to the back of it, just on the metal at the trunk. It doesn't look like anything but a tiny magnet, so it blends. I don't want to do it, but I think I need to. I need him to be innocent, and I need to prove he is. They're wrong, and I have to show them.

When he opens the door, Derek's face is pinched and his dark greenish-gray eyes are mostly gray. He looks cold and hard. "You okay?"

I shake my head, pausing on the cement. The light from inside shines behind him, taunting me with its warmth. I only have to sell my soul to the devil to go inside and be warm again.

He opens his arms for me. "You scared me."

I walk to him. Those arms are beacons of warmth and love. The only thing we've lost so far is the trust, but I think we might be able to get it back if I can prove he's innocent.

When I melt into them I feel different. I melt all the way without him forcing me. I pause, wondering if he feels it—the difference in me.

But he kisses the top of my head, smelling me. He hovers there, taking gulps of me like he has been starved all day of the life force I give off.

"I missed you all day. I was terrified. I thought I scared you away with the truth." He pulls me back. "Sam, I don't want to ruin what we have. You're my everything."

I shake my head. "Jane. Don't call me Sam."

He smiles, making everything okay. He blankets us in that smile and the love inside it, and I don't believe a single thing I read. I believe whatever he wants me to. He's perfect, and they're wrong. And when he leads me inside, kissing my cheeks and closing the door on us, I feel like he's closed the door on everything else. He's brought us into our safe haven and made us protected again.

I don't care about anything but that.

He drags my clothes off there at the door, stripping me naked, and scoops me up into his arms. He carries me to the bathroom and undresses himself, pulling us both into the shower. He protects me from the cold water until it's warm and then steps aside so I am blasted with heat. He wraps himself around me, letting the hot water wash it all away.

I close my eyes and breathe him in too, the same way he does me. I get it now—the dose he gets when he takes a breath pushes everything else away.

"Where did you go?"

I shake my head. "I rode the bus for a long time. Then I got a ride back with the cops. They were at a house on the outskirts of the city. So they drove me back, thinking I was a crackhead. I had to clear on the system before they would let me come home."

He kisses my neck. "Did you clear?"

"Yup. No Jane Spears in the system."

He pauses, mimicking the stiffened feel of my back. We are both aware of something suddenly, I just don't know what I'm aware of. I'm still lost, regardless of how my body reacts. "So, you never confessed to being Samantha Barnes?"

I turn to face him, looking up into his beautiful face. "I didn't. I don't think I am Samantha Barnes. I think she died a long time ago. I like being Jane. What good is going to come of being Samantha? She clearly has issues."

He drags his hand down my face, brushing his thumb against my lips. "I was so worried you hated me for lying to you."

I shake my head slowly. "I just needed to get some air and some distance. I needed to swallow the truth whole so I could digest the fact I've killed things in my sleep. That's haunting me. It makes me sick. I just think about the people looking for their animals that I've killed. It makes me ill."

His brow knits, and I see the hurt in his eyes. "It's not your fault. I swear, you are asleep. You don't know."

"We have to do something to make it stop."

He nods. "I will start sedating you again." He winces. "It's just—that's how you got into the accident last time. I sedated you and left the house. You got up, drove the car, and crashed it."

My wicked brain wonders if it's true. My eyes are mesmerized by his. They believe everything he says. But my brain whispers that there is no way a small, sedated woman got up and drove a car. If my scars are old, Derek is lying about it. But I want to give him the benefit of the doubt. I just don't know how far to follow him down this path, nodding my head like a smitten schoolgirl.

There is one thing I want to do, on the off chance everything Rory has said is true and my life is a complete lie. I lift my hands to his cheeks, cupping his face. I say the one thing I haven't ever said to him, not aloud. I have written it and texted it and whispered it when I thought he was sleeping. But I haven't ever said it. "I love you."

He winces. "Why did you say that?"

"Because you are everything I ever wanted in the world. I don't know how I know this. I don't remember ever wishing for you, but I know I did. In my soul and my being, I know I did."

He looks lost. "I love you, Jane. I always have."

I nod, believing it completely. "I know you have." And that's the truth of the matter. I know he has loved me since the dawn of our time.

I just don't know what to do with it.

7. GOING ROGUE

When we make love, I relax completely. I savor the feel of his body inside and on top of mine. The feel of him pressing me into the bed is magical.

The pill I pretend to swallow isn't.

He kisses me good night. I slip the pill into my pillowcase and close my eyes when he turns the light off.

I pretend to fall asleep, feigning the deep breathing and then the slack face. In the light of the alarm clock I can see him staring at me when I glance under my lashes. The look on his face is frightening. It's the first time I have ever seen anything like it. He looks detached from me completely.

After a while, I don't know how long, he climbs from the bed and dresses silently. Somewhere in the dark, my heart breaks with fear that he's actually the monster they say he is.

When he slips from the room I wait for the sound of the door closing to the outside before I sit up. Something immediately tells me to lie back down, so I do. I breathe deeply, suddenly afraid of every choice I have made. I lie there still and terrified, only to have it all confirmed by his sudden appearance as a silhouette in the doorway.

I don't hold my breath or inhale sharply, both movements I want to make. Instead, I continue to breathe as softly as I can. He stands there for a moment, a shadow in the doorway, before he turns and leaves the house for real.

I am near tears when I hear the car out front.

He either knew I was faking my sleep or suspected it. There's a real possibility he's a killer. Even in the warmth of our bed, I have to admit it.

I grab the pill and take it to the toilet, walking slowly through the dark room. I flush the pill, take a pee, and flush again. When I turn on the light it's gone, but I don't know how to continue with the plan I have formed in my feeble brain.

I get dressed quickly, pressing 911 on my phone as I walk out the front door in my all-black clothing. I feel like an idiot, but my body moves with stealth and my instincts are sharp.

"Tell me he's gone to work and ya need someone to keep that bed warm with ya!" Rory answers cheekily.

Ignoring his bravado I mutter, "He's left in the car."

"I know. I see the beacon moving on my screen. Come climb in." A black van down the road flashes me with its light as a door slides open. My insides twist and churn, but I walk to the van and climb in. Rory nods at me from behind a small laptop in the front passenger seat. "He's headed for Bellevue." A young man in the driver's seat starts the van and drives, jerking me back into a seat.

Rory nods at the young man, the only other occupant of the vehicle. "This is Antoine."

The young man waves back at me, glancing with dark eyes in the rearview. "Hi, Sam. We actually met eight years ago, but I know you don't remember me."

Rory hands me a black handgun. "You remember how to use this?"

I am about to say no when my hand reaches for it. The weight is more than familiar. I pull the clip, glance at it, and hammer it back in, in one smooth movement. Rory nods. "I'll go with yes."

Holding the gun is so foreign to me, and yet completely natural to my body. But my brain wins, and I start to hand it back to him. "I'd rather not have it, if it's all the same to you."

He shrugs. "It's not. I want you to have my back."

I turn, still holding the gun but pointing it at the floor. It trembles against my leg, weighing more and more by the second. I hold it by the handle, not going anywhere near the trigger.

"He's stopping. Chism Beach Park, it looks like." Rory turns, offering me a sympathetic look. "Ya know he's bad, right? Ya do understand that?"

I shake my head. "I know you think he's bad, but I've been with him for years. He hasn't ever been anything but perfect."

The sympathy leaves his face, replaced by disgust. "Ya don't really believe that, do ya? He's an evil man. He's conned ya."

Tension starts to build inside me. "You can't pretend to be amazing for years. He would have slipped up. I would have seen it."

"Love is blind, Sam. You see what you want."

There is no point in arguing. We're here for two different reasons. He wants Derek taken in on charges of murder. I just want Derek cleared so I can go back to my regular life. Whatever that is. When we cross the bridge my body starts to hum, vibrating with anxious energy and the bumpy ride of the van. There is a small part of me that's terrified of what we'll find. The other part of me assumes it'll be nothing.

But who leaves in the middle of the night after sedating his loved one? Who double-checks that his girlfriend is sleeping?

I know the answer to the question, but I refuse to believe in his guilt.

Antoine parks a mile from the beach and hops out. Rory jumps out with him, and they both give me a look. Rory is dressed in dark jeans and a black skintight jacket. It looks like Lululemon. His dark hair is styled perfectly, coiffed as if he were going on a date instead of a mission.

Antoine is the same. He looks about thirty and completely adorable. He's clearly Italian and I would imagine smooth in a dangerous way. The sort of guy who would be looking for love in all the wrong places.

Seeing them both reminds me of what Rory said to Angie. I scowl. "Why did you tell my friend you were looking for love in all the wrong places?"

"That was our code." He says it with a dirty smirk.

I cock an eyebrow, disgusted, as I step from the van, placing the gun on the seat when they're not looking, and close the door quickly.

They break into a run along the beach, making me wrinkle my nose and start after them with a slow jog. Rory glances back, shaking his head under a streetlight. "Haul some ass, Barnes."

I try to pick up the pace but get a cramp instantly and end up walking. Antoine turns back, jogging up to me. "Samantha Barnes walking? Damn, you *are* different." I'm gripping my side and wincing at the stitch when Antoine lifts my hands in the air, touching me like we know each other well. "Arms in the air, Barnes. A side stitch needs arms in the air." He walks next to me in the dark, nudging me a little. "You and Dash are fully together?"

"Derek, not Dash." I nod, feeling like a moron with my arms in the air but noticing the difference it's making.

"That's so nasty. He's insane."

"You don't know him."

Antoine gives me a skeptical stare with his dark eyes. "Trust me, if either of us is in the dark, it's not me." He grabs my hand and drags me into a run, much faster than my comfort level is set. When we get to the parking lot for the beach I'm winded and nauseated.

Rory glares at me from behind a tree. "Ya need to get in shape."

I take a knee, breathing like Ronald when he caught me. "I'm not in bad shape. I walk all the time. I just hate running."

Rory scoffs. "Since when? You were a track star in high school and college. You still hold the record for running the Cooper at basic."

I wipe my face, fighting the urge to wheeze and pass out. I'm exhausted and stressed. The whole superspy thing is too much work. I want to go back to bed and forget the whole thing.

Rory creeps ahead, constantly looking back to check on us. I follow Antoine, not being stealthy any longer. I'm ready to curl up under a tree.

"You okay?"

I nod. "I just feel like shit. Who runs at two in the morning? This is nuts."

He snorts. "It's like meeting your sweet yet lazy twin, I swear it. You were such a ball-busting bitch. This is almost refreshing."

I lift my middle finger in the air, something I'm not sure I've ever done. He rolls his eyes. "Never mind, looks like the old you is making a comeback."

"Whatever."

He points. "See, classic Sam." He grabs my hand and makes me run again. I want to whine and snivel and complain, but the reality of the situation is too dire.

"What are you, a cyborg?" I ask after we stop running and stand in a shadow.

Antoine grins, flashing his white teeth at me. "I was a marine for a year, then I got scouted by Randall. He came and asked if I'd be interested in something covert and top-secret security clearance—so top secret he couldn't tell me until I signed off on it. Of course I said yes."

"CIA?"

He nods. "Sometimes. Sometimes it's FBI, like now. This particular job is a joint task force between some of the local authority and the FBI. Secret Service is aware of it as well, since Dash killed three senators last year and we have to assume his target will be political."

"No, he didn't."

He nods. "He did. They were perfect too. One guy got shot with an icicle in the neck when he was away on an ice fishing holiday. It looked like the icicles had fallen from the cabin he was staying at, but the water in the icicles on the roof and the water found inside the wound were different. Just slightly, too, like he wanted us to see it. Then he killed another one in the man's own bed. Made it look like he'd had an allergic reaction, but there were traces of poison in his system that could be found only if he was tested two weeks after the murder. The poison is some jungle tincture that goes dormant, slowly releasing through the pores of the person over a two-week period. His skin was black—"

I put a hand up. "Okay, I don't care. I don't want to know that shit. It's nasty." I glance around at the empty lake and the still parking lot with nothing but Derek's car in it. Rory is using some magical binoculars to scope the scene out. There is nothing moving anywhere under the streetlights in the park or parking lot. I feel like I'm betraying Derek in every way, but if he knew I was here only to clear him, he might not hate me so much when he finds out. There is no *if he finds out*; I have a terrible feeling he already knows where I am. Losing him is still bigger than anything else, because no matter how I try to figure it all out, I can't see him being the killer they're seeking. I *can* see him being something for the CIA. He's brilliant and serious and exactly what a government agency would be looking for.

Rory comes back. "He's not here. No heat registering in this area for a mile."

Antoine pulls a cell phone out and makes a call, speaking softly. "You certain we have no one in this area who would be of interest to him?" He pauses, obviously listening to the person on the other side. His face twists. "FUCK!" He hangs up, looking fierce instead of smooth and sexy. "There's an ambassador to Jordan from Qatar in the area. His cousin lives nearby in Hunts Point. He's staying with him for a weekend before heading off to New York. No one knew he was here. The forms you fill out declaring the addresses you'll be at, this address was last on the list—he filled it out backward. According to it, he should be in New York this week, but the UN summit meeting is next week."

Rory turns, sprinting back toward the van. "Stay with her."

Antoine gives me a look. "You believe now?"

I shake my head.

He nods. "You will. When we get there this guy is gonna be dead in some twisted, sick, accidental-looking way. You wait." He sounds so smug and bitter. It's such a change from the funny guy he was ten minutes ago.

When the van comes tearing down the road to us, we hop in, and instantly they go to work—talking on cell phones and looking at screens, typing and texting. It's bananas to see people working in such a frenzy. Rory is shouting for a team to get in place with Derek's car and to apprehend him on the spot when he returns, while Antoine is looking up the address on a map. "The house is gated; no one can enter to knock on the door. It's a bell at the gate. We need a squad car there now—they need to wake the residents. We'll go in the side yard and sneak in the back door in case he runs." He hangs up and looks at me with the same severity as moments before. "You'd better be ready to bring it, Barnes, or you can sit in the van and wait."

"I want to wait."

Rory shakes his head, looking back at me while still driving. "No. She comes. He'll know she's here. She's at risk now."

I don't know the entirety of what that means. I have to assume he thinks I shouldn't be with Derek anymore. Like this is now me walking away from it all.

But I won't. I won't walk away from him. I love him and he loves me, and he isn't the man they're looking for. I don't care what they think. I know him.

The van stops with a jerk, and Rory hauls me out of the backseat, jamming my gun into my hands. "Don't pull that again. I'll smack ya around till ya remember who ya are."

I scowl at him, but he drags me to a large rock wall at least eight feet high, nodding his head toward it. I shake my head, but Antoine runs, leaping and climbing up the wall. I stuff the gun in the back of my pants, totally certain I'm going to shoot myself in the ass. He lowers his hand as Rory lifts me up.

Antoine drags me to the top of the wall, heights promptly becoming another item I realize is outside my comfort level.

Rory jumps up, climbing and dropping to the other side with no issue. Antoine shoves me. "Jump."

I shove him back. "DON'T!"

He tilts his head to the side. "You jump or I push."

I growl, feeling something spicy building inside me. I've gone along with this nonsense in hopes of showing them how wrong they are, but I'm getting tired of the bullshit. I sit on the wall, turning on my stomach and letting my legs hang over the edge. Slowly I lower myself down the wall, but Rory grabs me from below, dragging me before I'm ready. I drop, holding back my scream as he catches me. We are face to face, staring at each other in the dark. The dim light from the moon and streetlights flickers, making it so I can see he's looking me in the eye with an expression I'm not comfortable with. Slowly he lowers me down, making me slide down his body until I drop to the ground softly. His arms don't release me, but there is something I recall about him. I know him. I know this embrace and the smell of his body against mine.

Not that it matters. My heart still belongs to the man who has lovingly cared for me for years.

We creep along the side yard to the mansion. I pause, stunned by the beauty of the house before me. The few lights on inside glow like lanterns, lighting up the massive rooms inside the brick castle. The yard is the size of a city block, with grass all the way to the large dock at the bottom of the yard. Waterfront houses are usually fancy in this area, but I swear I have never seen any like this one.

"Who lives here?"

Antoine puts his finger to his lips. "Some rich guy from either Qatar or some other obscenely rich country."

"Damn!"

Rory grabs my arm roughly. "We aren't here for sightseeing, Sam. We need to find Dash before it's too late."

I jerk my arm free, annoyed at his constantly touching me. I don't think I've ever been big on touching. I follow them up the yard, staying behind the massive trees and bushes.

My heart should be in my throat. My stomach should be a concrete block, waiting to fall into my bowels and cause the worst diarrhea known to man. My palms should be sweating. My mouth should be cotton.

But none of those things are occurring. My heart hurts, but it's wholly for the dishonest thing I am doing to Derek. Maybe I'm an idiot, it's entirely possible, but I love him and he's never done a single thing to me besides lie because he was worried about me and wanted to protect us.

I can't fault Derek for any of it, especially not while I'm trespassing in a foreigner's yard trying to prove his innocence. I now understand how far he would go for me.

Rory opens the door to the basement, leading us into a billiards room with a massive bar and a large sitting area with leather couches and chairs. It's quite the room, considering it's the basement.

Our basement has boxes and old things Derek refuses to junk out.

Antoine and Rory have their guns out as we climb the stairs. In the house above, it sounds like people are being woken by the police. A woman is speaking quickly, flooding the silent air with emotional words in Arabic. She speaks, and slowly my mind filters the words through something. "She says they woke up and he was gone."

Rory glances back at me. "I know. Who do you think taught you Arabic?" I swallow hard, making him laugh. "You didn't know you could speak it?" I shake my head.

Antoine rolls his eyes, taking the steps until he meets a police officer. He flashes a badge. "Is the ambassador in the house?"

The young cop shakes his head, confused at how we are here already.

"Any sign of a struggle?"

"No," he answers, glancing back up the stairs. "We searched everything. Looks like he walked out the front door. Didn't take a car."

I cock an eyebrow smugly. "Well, we know he wasn't with Derek then. His car is still parked."

The cop's confused look worsens. Rory points at me. "Ignore her, it's her first rodeo."

They all laugh, but I miss the joke. The Arabic woman speaking has my attention again. "She says he wasn't feeling well at dinner. He was thinking about going to the doctor."

Rory grabs my hand, dragging me up the stairs, past the cop. We hurry back to the road where the van is parked.

The ride to the hospital is silent. I don't know what to add to the awkwardness of the empty air, other than more awkwardness, so I don't speak. Instead, I gaze out the window as we cross Evergreen Point Bridge, heading back into the city.

Antoine parks the van in front of the emergency entrance of the hospital Derek works at. My stomach tightens. *Did they know he worked here?*

As we climb out, I abandon my gun again, watching them pocket theirs. It seems weird to take a gun into a hospital.

Rory storms to the emergency nurses' station, asking them things in a near whisper and flashing his badge. The nurse at the front desk looks confused for a moment, but her computer gives them an answer. Her face lights up as she points, smiling at him in a way that makes me want to warn her. He speaks to Antoine for a moment before he places his hand at the base of my spine, controlling the direction and speed of my gait.

I wish for a half second I had brought the gun. When the elevator doors close and we are alone, I shove Rory back, sticking a thin finger in his face. "Touch me again and I break whatever is making contact with me."

It doesn't make him angry to be threatened. It makes him do the opposite of everything I want. He steps into me, pressing his chest against mine. "Ya might not remember how much ya like it when I touch you, but I remember. Just because ya lost your memory and forgot how much ya love me doesn't mean I have to forget how much I love ya." He dips his face, banking on the fact his words have stunned me still, and presses his face against mine.

My knee comes up, but he anticipates it, so I bite. He cries out as a rusty taste fills my mouth. I shove him back, shaking my head. "I mean it."

He nods, licking his lip and grinning like a psycho. "Me too, Sam. I love you. Always have, always will."

I turn, looking back at the door as it opens. "You don't even know me. And stop calling me Sam. My name is Jane."

He leans against the doorway, blocking me in. "Trust me, Jane, you are not who you think you are!"

I shake my head. "You don't know me."

His face changes into a grim smirk. "Baby, if I don't know you, you're fucked."

There is a horrible feeling inside me that he's telling the truth. There's a familiarity between us that screams of a history of intimacy.

He turns and stalks off the elevator, walking with swag that almost forces me to check his ass out. For a cheeky Irishman, he's fine. But that just adds more conflict over the whole backstory he's given me. I'm susceptible to advertising. I think I always have been, and I don't want to believe him because he's attractive. I want proof.

Imagining the two of us together makes me think I must have fallen for his body, because his charms are lacking in every way.

I shudder at the image of his foul mouth touching mine again.

There's no way we were ever in love. Whatever we had must have been based on sexual chemistry alone.

When he gets to the large nurses' station for the floor, he leans across the desk to talk to the ladies. I am nearly there when I notice one I've met before. I spin before she sees me, running back to the elevator. I don't want Derek's coworkers to tell him I was here. I press my back against the wall and wait. When all this is over I'm going to wear my red dress and come to the Christmas party. I want everything to go back to the way it was.

Rory comes back moments later. "The ambassador is in a coma. He's gone into organ failure and is on life support."

I scoff. "That could be from anything."

"And I'm psychic enough to predict it?"

I don't have an argument for that. He has a point. "I want to go home."

"He hasn't gone back to his car yet. He's not home. We need to apprehend him before you can leave our custody."

"That means nothing. I want to go home because I need to be asleep for real when he gets there. Not dressed in all black and roaming the streets with you two idiots. He isn't your man. I'm telling you."

He rolls his eyes, pressing the button for down. When we get back downstairs, the hallway is filled with men in suits and police. We walk through them all, not briefing any of them on the situation. I assume they all know the details.

At the end of the dimly lit hallway we find Antoine talking to a tall man with an angry face. He scowls when he sees me. "I didn't believe it. You have to be on your last life."

This has quickly become my least favorite thing ever, the whole *they remember me and I remember nothing.*

"Randall, she's back. No questions about before. It doesn't matter—she doesn't remember anyway."

His steely eyes narrow. "I have some testing scheduled for her first. Take her to a safe house until we can test her."

Rory nods. "The ambassador is dying, you should know."

He sighs, glaring at me viciously. "You should have brought him in, Sam. I'm not happy about this shit."

Antoine shakes his dark head. "We had nothing. We still have nothing."

Randall sighs a second time. "Well, we've been told he's no longer of interest to us anyway."

"He just killed a dignitary from another country."

Randall laughs bitterly. "Oh, you don't have to tell me. We've run this op for seven years. He's killed a hundred people. He's vanished like a ghost with one of ours and erased her mind. He's playing with us, and the higher-ups feel that he's one of two things. He's either a spook assassin we aren't being told about because his pay grade is so high that even the president doesn't need to know, or he's more dangerous with us to torment. They think he kills more frequently when we actively pursue him."

"You're fucking with me, right?"

Randall shoots Rory a look. "I want you on the next flight back to DC, where we will all regroup."

I can feel panic starting to build in me. "What if I don't want back in? I don't remember anything anyway."

"Sam, we haven't wanted you back. Rory said you were eager to catch Dash in action. He said you wanted revenge." Randall snorts.

I cock an eyebrow. "He told me I would be charged with treason if I didn't play along."

Randall shakes his head. "You're free if you want out, but this is it for you. The end of the line."

"Done."

Rory grabs my arm. "Wait. You wouldn't want this. The real you—she wouldn't want you to stay trapped in there with him. You wanted him behind bars."

I jerk free, shoving him back. "I want you all out of my life. That's what I want. Sam Barnes is dead. Let's leave her there."

Randall nods at the door. "I have a car; I'll give you a ride. You two go to the airport. The jet is there. I'll meet you."

Rory looks like he might argue again, but he doesn't. I don't look back to see the angry stare he's trying to kill me with. I push out into the night air and climb into the black car with Randall. A man drives but doesn't look back at us.

Randall speaks softly, "You can't blame him, Sa— Jane. He's been devastated and searching for you for six years. Everyone figured you would be in Europe, so he's been there working but looking for you the entire time. Every time a politician or figurehead even coughs or farts, he blames Benjamin Dash. He's been searching for you high and low."

"Maybe I didn't want to be found."

"Maybe you shouldn't have let Rory fall in love with you."

I turn and nod. "You're right. I never should have let him love me, but I don't remember being that girl. I don't care who Benjamin

Dash is. I care that I am Jane Spears. I am a shopgirl. I am happy and stress free. Since all of this started washing back up in my life, I've been stressed. I feel funny in my skin for the first time in years. I don't think Sam was a good person, and I don't want to be her. I don't want her baggage or her bullshit."

The car stops at a red light, and I see my store. "I'll get out here." I open the door and walk out into the night. I take my usual route home. My cell phone rings in my pocket, making me nervous Derek is home, but when I answer, it isn't his voice screaming in my ear. It's Rory.

"He's not with that car in Bellevue. It wasn't his car we were tracking. He must have known you put the tracker on and dumped it on another silver Mercedes. The guy just got back—he's a rower. That means—"

"He's home and waiting for me." I finish his sentence. Dread and guilt battle for the top spot in my emotions.

"Where are you? I'll come get you."

"No. Go to the airport. He won't hurt me." I hang up the phone and walk behind the building to the street where our house is. Seeing his car makes me gag a little, but I keep walking. I force my steps. Every inch of me wants to run except my heart. My heart drags my feet across the street and up the driveway.

I open the unlocked door, peeking into the darkness. The silent house is still. Even Binx stays hidden. My stomach is in my throat as I close the door, pressing my back against it. Images of him rampaging with a knife in his hand flicker through my mind. I turn the lock on the door, slipping my shoes off. I walk into the kitchen first. It's dark, with the pale-blue glow of the appliances the only light. I walk into the dining room, but he isn't in there.

So I turn to the living room, but again it's empty.

This isn't me. I have been drawn into their madness, locked away in their fears, and let them rule me. I believe I am safe in my home with my boyfriend. But strangers have me scared by all the what-ifs.

I swallow hard, tiptoeing past the French doors that face the backyard to the hallway where the bedrooms are.

When I open the door to our room, I notice the sweat on my palms as I turn the handle. In the glow of the moonlight and street-lights, I see him sitting in the chair like Norman Bates. His silhou-ette and the shadow he casts are more frightening than a single thing I have done in the past couple of days.

I close the door, leaning against it and trapping us both in the dark.

"Did you come to kill me?" His voice is soft and yet strong, not defeated as his shadow on the floor might suggest.

"No." Shit. My heart is breaking as the silence and simple words become all the proof I ever needed.

He lifts his face, showing me his eyes as they reflect the light from the window. "You must know their version of everything."

"No." The words are a lie, but I want nothing like I do our peace and to return to our life.

He stands, making every hair on my body stand on edge, and crosses the floor slowly. His steps are soft and deliberate. When he reaches me I swear I see him hesitate. "Do you know my name?"

My stomach sinks as I nod, feeling a single tear slip down my cheeks. There is a terrible feeling inside me that facing him is like facing a wild animal.

"Say it."

Glancing up into his beautiful face I say the name I want to say. "Dr. Derek Russo."

A smile crosses his lips, but it's not the one I love. It's bitter and filled with what I fear is the end of us. "Say it." He doesn't specify. He doesn't have to.

I swallow hard, letting the words fall out of my lips. "Benjamin Dash."

"And who are you?"

A sound leaves my lips. It's defeat in its simplest form. "Jane Spears."

"Liar." He lifts his hand, running it through my hair and then cupping my cheek. He leans forward, I assume to kiss me, but he whispers in my ear instead: "Who are we?"

I shake my head. "I don't know." My response is a whisper to match his.

"We are the hunter and the prey." He kisses my cheek softly. "Which one are you, Samantha Barnes?"

I close my eyes, no longer fearing him, regardless of the fact I am certain he is every bit the man Rory said he was. "My name is Jane."

"What are you doing here? Why didn't you leave?"

"I told you earlier, I love you. I have always loved you. I don't want us to be this way. I don't believe you are anything but my sweet Derek." I know it's wrong, but I don't care that he's an assassin. He might have killed a man tonight—he's all but admitting to it all, and I don't care.

His lips find mine in the dark. There is something desperate in the kiss. There is no control and no method to his madness; it is just pure and crazed.

His fingers tear at my clothes, where his lips press to heal the reddened flesh. He kisses away every bit of roughness but never softens in his touch. My clothes are ripped away completely as my lips are kissed as though they may never be again. I don't move with him but allow myself to be ravaged. I am unsure of his mood or movements. Everything is foreign and frightening in a sensual way.

He lifts me into the air, lowering me onto his erection. His jeans rub the bottoms of my legs as he enters me roughly. His hands lift me by the hips and ass, working me on his cock but at the same time moving with abandon on the reins normally holding him back. Warm grunts fill my ears as my head and back drag up and down the door. His fingers bite into my flesh, holding me too tightly and treating me too roughly. But I love every second of the assault.

Our lips crash as our faces melt into one another. My tongue slips into his mouth, only to be met with caresses and soft sucks, contradicting the thrusting and slamming of my body.

My naked breasts squish into his shirt in rhythm to the jerking of our bodies as my climax starts to build. I grip him, clutching and clawing as his cock brings me to a blissful release. He cries out, groaning into my hair as my orgasm milks his cock until he too releases inside me. Our movements slow but the disparity of it all doesn't.

He doesn't hesitate. He moves our still-trembling bodies, carrying me to the shower. He strips off his clothes, pulling me into the shower. He turns it on, as always, protecting me from the cold water.

He cups my face as if it were the most delicate thing in the world. His eyes are almost completely gray, no green at all, but his smile is the one I love the most. "I don't want to lose you."

I nod. "Can we just be who we are, right now? These people in this shower?"

His eyes glisten, and I know it's not the shower. "I don't know." He kisses me softly, just lightly feathering his lips against mine. "I have never been more scared in all my life than I was today."

I nod again. "Me too."

He wraps around me, holding me tightly to his chest.

When we go to bed there are a thousand questions roaming my head, but choosing which one to start with feels impossible. Each one leads down a path I'm not certain I want to detour down. Not when he's here and he's mine.

I hate myself in some ways. I hate that I needed to know. I hate that I followed the bread crumbs to Samantha Barnes and the bullshit that was her life. I wish I'd left it alone. I wish for so many other options instead of the one that led me to the moment I am in. It is too filled with regret, so filled that I'm certain if I break the top off this can of worms I will drown in the sea of things I could have lived without knowing.

"Do you want me to sedate you?" His question is so random I don't answer at first. I lie perfectly still, perplexed as to why he would ask it.

"No." I almost answer as if I'm asking a question.

He turns, facing me. I can hardly make out his face in the dark. "You might sleepwalk."

"I thought you made that up."

He shakes his head, rustling it against the pillow. "No. You really killed a cat in front of me. You really sleepwalk. You really wake covered in blood—not often, but you do."

"You didn't do that to me?"

It's his turn to sit in silent contemplation. I regret asking it, even more so when he answers.

"I have done everything I can to make you safe. I have told you a thousand times that I love you. You have always been my priority, even when you didn't know me. The first chance you are given something that could make you doubt me, and you believe that, over the years of love and sacrifice? How did it take such a small thing to make you doubt me when it was so hard to make you love me?"

My insides clench. "I don't know what to believe. I don't know what to think about the sleepwalking. I don't think I did it when I was a kid."

He gets up abruptly, bringing instant panic out in me. He walks from the room, flooding the hallway with light and heavy footsteps. He bangs and clangs and rifles through things downstairs in the concrete basement.

It's then that I realize how little I know about him, and it makes me trust him even less, if at all. I have a fear that he's downstairs making something that will be my demise.

A realization hits me like a shovel to the face: Our love will never work. He will always be a suspect in my brain that is naturally on the side of the law, even though I never knew it was. I am naturally skeptical, even if I am lost in the mud and fog in my head. I wish I could take it all back. I wish for a second I could just be the girl with no memories again.

His heavy footsteps leave the basement as he rushes back into the room. He looks me over, giving me the strangest face. I can hardly make it out with the light of the hallway behind him. He starts to speak softy, but I'm lost in the look on his face. I think it's defeat, but I can't be certain.

I don't hear what he's saying, not completely. I just watch him, hating how beaten and rough he looks. It's more than tired and stressed. It's loss in its simplest form. He is losing me and I am losing him, and we both know it.

I fear it puts me in a sticky situation, though, what with him being the serial killer and me being the ex-agent of sorts. I don't think either of those roles defines us, but our love doesn't either. Not anymore.

My doubt in him is a betrayal of the worst kind. It matches his lies, even here in the dark where we can't see everything and we say nothing that will patch these injuries.

He drops to his knees, and I realize he's holding a box. He's telling me things I don't listen to. The box has become my focus. Its contents drive my curiosity.

He struggles with words for a moment, taking a deep breath. "Your name is Samantha Barnes. You were an agent assigned to bring me in." I watch him slip away, fading as a person and becoming a shell, a husk. He is empty when he says his next words. "I was also an agent, assigned to something different. Killing people is an art, one only a certain type of person can stomach." He blinks and breathes and looks pained in some way, but he is a robot. I see that now. "I was a doctor in the military—easiest way to become one without paying for it. I didn't have money growing up." There is something else to his story of growing up that I can see is there in his hollow eyes. There is pain there that he has buried with the deaths of others.

My skin shivers. How is all this possible?

I pull back from him, distancing myself from his words as he continues to speak softly, as if the quiet of his voice will mask the horror of his words. "The CIA recruited me when I was twenty-five. I became a cleaner." He lifts his face, smiling blankly. "I loved my job." He winces. "Until I was assigned a girl, a woman named Samantha Barnes. I came to your town, watched you and researched you. I met your father and your aunt. I met every person I could find who knew you, but every piece of the puzzle and every step of the way made me feel something I didn't understand. I found myself watching you for hours. Simple things like sleeping and eating and even bathing. I became obsessed with every aspect of who you were. I realized then I was in love with you. I couldn't kill you any more than I could kill myself." His words and unsteady grip on the box fill me with fear. A new type of fear, one I have never felt.

My head moves back and forth slowly, refusing to believe anything he says.

He offers me a weak look. "When I found out I was set up and you were my mark so you could bring me in, I was devastated. You were bait, a trap. The CIA had no more need of me. I'd been seen, recognized by someone. They didn't want me dead, they wanted me alive."

I laugh, aghast and confused. "That's ridiculous. Why would they want you alive?"

"They knew if I died the world would know everything I knew." His eyes narrow. "I've always been one to keep insurance policies on the jobs I've done. They know me too well to kill me off without a guarantee that I'm not leaking information to the wrong people."

I shake my head. "I don't understand what any of this has to do with how we got here."

He switches on the bedside lamp, places the box in my lap, and gets up, leaving the room. I stare at it, unable to move for a moment. The name on it is Samantha Barnes.

Lifting a shaky hand, I open it, only to be increasingly stunned and scared by its contents. Truly scared.

The first image is like meeting a twin sister for the first time, after twenty years of separation. The girl looks like me, but she can't be me. There is no way.

She has blonde hair and so much makeup on that it scares me, literally. Her face is perfect and glossed with enough makeup to frost a cake. The second photo is black-and-white, and even still I can see she isn't me. There is no way. She looks loud and cocky, just with her expression. The confidence and air of her is smarmy—something I don't think I could be, even if I were acting. Her thin body has hardly a stitch of clothing on, and shoes that look like they would break a back. She is walking through an alley, holding her sunglasses and staring back at someone, the photographer, maybe. She looks like she is about to smile or she knows a secret. I shake my head, muttering into the dim light, "That's not me."

Flipping through the photos is like watching a movie, one I couldn't possibly be the star of, and yet there I am. Blonde, brunette, redhead. They are like the photos in the folder Rory gave me, but worse. These are of me on jobs, real jobs. There are photos of me not working too. Ones where I am sitting in a café with no makeup and hair in a ponytail, contemplating life and whatever else a girl like that thinks about. He has shots of me washing dishes in my kitchen and sleeping in my bed.

It makes me sick to think I didn't know. He was always there.

The last thing in the box is a camera. It's small and cheap look-ing. I turn it on, clicking through the photos. They're all of him. He has very dark hair and a paler complexion. He looks like he's from the East Coast in these photos. He's walking and eating and drinking and reading. He's in hotels and a house, and I see now I invaded his space as much as he did mine. I was watching him and he was watching me, and I suspect we might have fallen in love this way, through a lens.

I flip to the next picture, but it's a video, not a photo. My body grows cold as I press "play" and brace myself for the unknown.

The video starts with me recording myself. My hair is bright blonde, and I have dark-red lipstick on. I lick my lips and whisper, "I don't know what's going to happen, but you need to do this. You need to choose love or a job. If you're watching this, then you've discovered who we were. I'm sorry for that. It's not a perfect world, and the possibility you would find out was always there." My eyes have a look in them, a look like I am desperate, but I don't believe the emotions behind the expression. "You love him, and you want to become someone new, trust me. I want Samantha Barnes to die." Old me smiles at the camera, and I don't believe a word she's spoken. She looks behind her, nervously. But I can see she's holding the camera up to show something beyond the face she's making. She's showing me something. She looks back. "Don't ever go back. Trust me." The video ends, and I am convinced she wants me to go back. *I* want me to go back. I just don't know where back is, but I do know the look in those eyes. Something about this video changes everything. I place the camera back in the box, overwhelmed and scared.

He comes back into the room, kneeling in front of me and placing a cold hand over mine. "I'm sorry you have to go through this. Neither of us ever wanted you to find out. We wanted a fresh start."

"Why did you lie when I started figuring it out?" My words are breathy and weak.

He squeezes my hand. "Jane, we wanted you to stay hidden from that world. We both wanted to be free of the people we were. Neither of us ever wanted the past to catch up with us. We knew it was possible, but we didn't want it."

"But you continued killing people, even after the fresh start?"

"It's not something I could quit." He has no excuse for himself. "Not even for you. Believe me, I tried. Going back to it is what kept us both alive."

My mouth is dry and my heart is pounding. I shake my head, not even wanting to talk about his murders or what kept me alive. "How did you do it? How did you take my memories?" I change the subject.

He nods. "Surgery. We performed a surgery to mimic a brain injury and give you amnesia. I'm so sorry. I wish to God we never had to have this conversation." His face is sad and guilty.

"You operated on my brain? That's the scar on my head at the back?"

He presses his lips and finally speaks softly. "We have to do it again. We can't stay here. We have to start over again. That's what you said. If you ever found out, you wanted us to start over again."

The reality of the situation and what he's threatening me with make my eyes water. He is going to make it all go away again. As much as I wished for it only moments ago, now that I'm faced with it, I don't think I want that. I don't know what to do.

He shakes his head. "Don't think about it tonight, just try to get some sleep. We'll leave tomorrow. I've made certain we won't be followed this time." His eyes suddenly have come alive with hope and something else that sparkles in the dim light. "Do you still love me, Jane?"

I want to shove him back and scream that he's not my boyfriend and I never want to see him again. I want to panic and freak out that he's performed some kind of brain surgery on me and sedated me every night. I want to do a thousand things, but I don't get the chance.

He swallows. "Baby, I'm still me, and you are you. I still love you."

My lower lip trembles. "Are you sure you understand what love is?" The words are harsh, and considering the things I now see are wrong with him, they might have been a mistake.

"I can't live without you."

I want to tell him I don't imagine I'll live long *with* him. I want to tell him several things that never leave my lips.

"Do you love me?" He asks it as if he's confused. I don't answer because I can't. I do love him, but I don't want this. I don't want to have brain surgery and have my mind erased again. He nods slowly, backing away from me. "Don't worry, baby, I can love you enough for both of us." He says it with a smile, but that doesn't take the chill off the true meaning in the sentence.

I turn my face to the window as he closes the door. I see how it is with clarity like I never have before. I now see I will never get away.

Not without killing him first.

He's too smart and too thorough, and I'm afraid he's in control, even when I think he's lost it. In my mind, if he had wanted a fresh start he would have stopped killing. To top it all off, I don't believe I made that video for any reason other than to give myself a clue without being obvious.

8. SEE JANE RUN

He doesn't sleep with me. He gives me space, or holds me hostage. I'm not sure which it is. But the moment I hear him snoring on the couch, I am up instantly and pulling on my clothes. I leave the nightgown in the bed on the pillows I stuff and pull up. It looks like I am sleeping, but maybe a little chubbier. I turn the lock on the door softly, listening to the hallway for a moment.

When I hear nothing but his snoring, I grab my phone and creep to the window, opening it and looking out. I toss my slippers onto the grassy ground of our backyard below.

The wind comes in the window, pushing me back. I sigh, hating the second-story height, and climb up onto the sill. The ledge is narrow and the wind is strong.

I grip the siding with my sweaty palms and shuffle with my bare feet along the chilly ledge. The wind pushes at me, flipping my hair and ruffling my clothes—and sanity. My hands slide along the cold building until I get to a corner. I climb along the corner to where there is a roof below me. It's the one over the basement stairs. I take a breath, force away my disbelief, and jump the fifteen feet down to the grass. My knees buckle, and I roll until I'm lying on my belly, nearly kissing the filthy grass. I can't believe I made it out. Getting up quickly, I jog to my slippers and slip around the far side of the yard to the fence. It backs onto a huge apartment complex. I run through the parking lot to a garage.

My feet hardly make a sound as I creep into the garage. I lift the door handles on the cars parked in there until one makes a clicking sound that is like angels singing to me. I sit in the driver's seat and look at the steering wheel, running my hands up and down it. Nothing comes back to me. I remember the movies I've seen and look around the car, flipping the visor and feeling around the different places, but there is no key. I sigh and glance down where there should be a keyhole, but there isn't one. Instead, there's a strange button with the word "start." I press the button and the engine starts, making me almost jump out as I look around for the owner of the car. After a minute with no one coming, I back the car out of its space and down the quiet street, assuming it's a remote starter of sorts.

I look down at the starter button, shaking my head. *What moron puts a push start in an unlocked car?*

The question is answered a mile down the road when the car randomly stops. It must have a radius it can run in but stops when the key is no longer in range.

I run along the streets of the residential area, lifting the door handles on every car I pass until I come across one that opens. I climb in, letting my mind go blank, and reach down, tearing the wiring and spark-starting it like a criminal. Wait—that's not the term for it. Hot-wiring. I can hot-wire!

Jesus!

I drive as far as the car will go, four hours out of Seattle. The car runs out of gas in the city limits of Spokane. I leave it on the side of the road and start the trek to the city. I am exhausted and starving again by the time I get within a few blocks of the downtown area.

I have no money, no food, no clothes, and no shoes. I am on the run, but I'm not sure what I'm running from or to.

I bite my lip and look around the street, catching a glimpse of myself in the window of the store I am next to. My image distorts, and I see her, the blonde. She smiles at me, dangling a cherry from her lips. She takes a bite of it. It's seductive and ballsy. Neither of which I am.

I need to go back. I don't even know where back is, but I need to go there. She was trying to tell me something. I pull my phone from my pocket and dial 911. It's the only option I can reasonably think of.

"Miss me already?" I can see the smug-ass grin on his face just by hearing his voice.

"Rory, I'm in trouble."

He scoffs. "I coulda told ya that." He chuckles, but I can tell it's an exhausted laugh. "Sam, where are ya?"

"Spokane."

"I'll be there in three hours. Can you hold tight? Meet me at the bus station, and ditch that phone. He's tracking it for sure." He hangs up, leaving me there with that. Nothing, really.

He won't be here for hours, and I'm stuck in a city with no food.

But I'm not the feeble girl I was a week ago.

I'm a survivor.

I turn and drop the phone off the bridge I'm on and walk up a street called S Coeur Dalene St. It's a bit dodgy at the bottom near the bridge, but as I climb the hill it gets better. When the concrete changes to red bricks, the houses become a mixture of stunning and estate-like or small family homes. The area looks like it once was older but now is being upgraded with newer and bigger homes. I find a house with no cars out front and no people walking about, making shadows inside. I don't look around like I'm guilty. I just walk into the backyard like this is my house or I have directions from the owners. The backyard is immaculate, much like those of the other houses in the neighborhood would be.

I walk to the small patio and open the door. Of course it opens. It's a smaller city, with trusting people. I hurry to the kitchen, making no noise in my slippers. The fridge is filled with all kinds of options, making me nearly giggle as I take the first bite of the apple I steal. The juice bursts in my mouth. I don't know the last time I ate so I fill up on pepperoni, cheese slices, and yogurt cups. I drink from the juice jug like a savage, spilling the orange juice down my face a little.

My stomach is overly full when I put everything back and wipe down the cupboards and floor where I spilled. I hurry, exploring the house silently but stopping when I find the mudroom and open the dryer, taking a pair of yoga pants out. They're a bit big, but it doesn't matter. I drag them on with a T-shirt and a sweater and pull on socks before closing the dryer. Holding my dirty clothes, I contemplate bringing them before I shrug and place them in the hamper.

The closet has a dozen jackets, all for a woman a touch larger than me, but it's perfect for the extra layers. I put on a coat and hiking boots; at least they fit perfectly. I leave through the garage next to the mudroom and out the side door into the front yard.

I don't know how long it'll take me to walk to the downtown area; not knowing Spokane well is a bit of a hindrance. We've come here twice since moving to Seattle. But I believe I know where the bus station is, having seen it once. We parked our car behind a building across the street from it.

I head down the hill, back to the overpass and bridge area. The traffic is slower than when I arrived, as midmorning has hit and the rush is over. The sidewalk on Sunset Boulevard is cracked and broken. It isn't at all like the other Sunset Boulevard I've walked on. It's a bit sketchy, and I'm glad it's midmorning and not late at night.

West Sunset isn't much of an improvement. It's all very underdeveloped and messy. It makes me miss Seattle.

I miss me. I miss being blind.

When I get onto West Second, the street becomes a touch more inviting. My heart races a bit less as I make my way into what feels more like the start of the downtown area.

No matter how unfamiliar and foreign the place is to me, I hate that I feel his eyes on me at every turn. I don't know if I will ever feel safe again. Seeing the pictures of me, I realize he won't ever stop looking for me. If I want this to end I have to kill him or bring him in, but I don't think I can do either. So my only other option is to run, even when I want to go back so badly it hurts.

There is a sick longing for him inside me, but I run my fingers along the scar on my head and remind myself of the lengths he went to in making me his. Not to mention the frightened look in my eyes on the video. Something was very wrong there. Worst-case scenario, in his drive to be with me, I have to assume there may be a possibility he would murder me to prevent me from leaving.

I don't understand why I am here. Why Samantha Barnes would have ever chosen this as a fate. Why she would have ever agreed to a near lobotomy. There is a chance Samantha Barnes didn't agree to any of it. I have to see that.

But any way I try to solve it, the only way to the answers is in going back.

The bus station takes me a half hour to get to. It's easy to find when you spot the bus drivers in their uniforms walking about, to and from work.

I lean against the wall in an obscure corner of the bus station, like a panhandler, and wait. My eyes never stop looking for him. The conflict of his finding me is too much for one person to struggle with. I want him to and I don't. It's not an even tie. The rational side of my brain agrees he's insane and I am on borrowed time as far as being with him is concerned. But the hopeless, feeble dipshit I was with him wants him back. I want to be loved and protected. It was easy with him, always.

And he had a point when he said that his actions for years should have outweighed the words spoken against him.

If he is sick, his disease is clearly managed by his work with the CIA. Unless he's been killing people Rory doesn't know about. It's scary that he obviously thinks he needs to kill people, but it's even scarier that I'm trying to look past it. Yet he has never done anything but love me.

My butt aches nearly as badly as my mind and heart do, but I don't move. I just watch as people come and go in hordes. Boarding and departing buses and trams. It's a crowded place.

A man comes and sits next to me, grinning broadly. "Hey, Jane!"

I almost smile when I see Antoine in a hoodie and sweats. He looks gangsta but he's still sexy as sin on a stick.

"Ready to get out of here?"

I nod, getting up and following him out into the crowd. My legs are cramped and aching, but it feels good to be moving. He walks to a small black SUV with tinted windows. The back door opens as we near it. I climb in to find Rory sitting in the backseat.

"Hello, love."

I scowl, not completely convinced he's the right person to be trusting. He offers me a bag with donuts in it. I stuff a whole one in my mouth, savoring the sweetness of the glaze as I devour it.

Antoine gets into the driver's seat, starting and driving off. I turn to the right to look out the window and see Derek standing in the doorway I have just come from, watching me. He wanted me to see him, or I wouldn't have. I don't say a word, just swallow my lumping mouthful and force my aching heart to shut the hell up, even if my brain won't.

He followed me the entire way. Was he protecting me?

9. BAD JUJU

The house is small and dumpy, one of the worst in the tiny little town of Geneva, Alabama. I had demanded that they take me back before I would help them. Rory was certain my father's house was as far back as everything went. In fact, he was insistent we come here. Now I'm not so sure. I glance at Rory skeptically. "You sure?"

He nods. "This was your dad's house. You brought me here once, drove past it. Your dad had just died, terrible way to go. You refused to go to the funeral but drove me past the house." His words feel like lies. Why wouldn't I have gone to the funeral? He was my father, even if he was a sucky one.

I climb out of the SUV, closing the door quietly, I think so I won't stir the ghosts sleeping here. I get the distinct feeling this house is haunted.

My footsteps sound like they echo as I approach the dirty little house. It's pale blue, with only one window in the front by the door. There's been a "For Sale" sign in the window for years, but it's never sold. I still own it, technically. I have for seven years.

My fingers clutch the filmy, rusted handle on the porch door, holding it back so Rory can insert the key. The real estate office has been the caretaker for it since I was gone. The lock clinks like an old chain, and when he gets the door open I nearly gag on the smell. "No wonder it never sold. It's dank and musty in there."

He glances back at me with a story playing out in his eyes, but I don't know it. I just recognize the look of it. We enter the small living room, and instantly something bad happens to my body. Something crippling and suffocating. There are ghosts here, memories that haunt the house, and I know now I don't want them back. There is something here that made me the girl I was. The girl with the cherry in her mouth, the bleached-blonde hair, and the haunted eyes—she is a product of this dank and haunted house. I take as many steps backward as I had taken forward until I am again on the stoop.

He looks back at me, tilting his head. "Still a no then?" He sounds annoyed with me.

I nod, backing up even farther. I would never have hidden any answers in this place. I wouldn't have come here. I can feel that truth pumping through my blood and body. When we get back in the car he doesn't speak, but I know he plays out an entire conversation in his mind. There is something I'm missing. "Where does my aunt Pat live?"

He glances at me. "North Carolina. She's still there, but you never saw her, ever."

I nod. "I want to see her."

"It's going to take all day to get to Charlotte."

"I don't care. I want to go."

He sighs, nodding. "Fine, but you're driving at least some of the way. I'm exhausted."

"Fine." It dawns on me that we sound like an old married couple. I have some level of comfort that's subconscious with him. I see it now. I don't act on my best behavior, and I say far more than I ever would with anyone else. Maybe even with Derek.

The drive isn't as long as he said it would be; it's just less than seven hours. We stop and get coffee twice and gas once, but it isn't so long that I'm dying or twitchy from sitting.

I worry more about meeting my aunt than anything.

"Does she know my memory is gone?" I ask, after letting it all plague me for hours. He stirs, not opening his eyes, but answers. He's been trying to sleep since I started driving at the halfway point.

"No. She thinks you died."

"WHAT!"

He nods sleepily and stretches. "Yeah. We told her your plane went down. There was an accident at the time. It made sense to use it."

"She thinks I'm dead, and you didn't tell me?"

He opens one dark-blue eye like a cat might. "Ya didn't ask."

I swat him. It's a knee-jerk reaction, and I regret doing it the moment my hand makes contact with his arm. But he laughs like I've hit him a thousand times. "I can't believe you were going to let me go there and not tell me."

He nods at the road, adjusting himself in his seat. "I woulda said something down the road a little ways. She's going to be excited to see ya. She loved ya something fierce."

When we drive into Charlotte he points. "This road, take a right, and drive to the end." The road is long and straight through an industrial section and then leads us through an older section of town. "Left at the stop sign." The moment we are sitting at the stop sign at the end of South Mint Street, my mouth goes dry. Wood-crest Avenue rings so familiar in my head that I glance up the road, knowing I can see the house.

"Second house on the right."

It's small and green with broken front steps and a small porch out front. I park on the road in front of the house, not sure if I should move or not. The broken planters in the grass make me sad. "She must be depressed to let it look this way."

He nods. "I imagine she has been sad for years." I leave the car running and climb out. I hurry to the front door, skipping the first step like always. I know what her face will look like. Her lips are puckered from smoking. She's the lady who sang in the car. She's the only real memory I have from before. I knock, not worrying if she will be angry with me.

I know she will understand. It's who she is.

There's movement in the tiny house, and the door cracks slowly, as if she's nervous about who might be there. Her eyes are the same as I recall, dark blue and light like mine. She and my mother both had it.

She looks confused at first, lost in the face she sees. But the moment she realizes what is happening she steps back, clutching at her own throat. She gasps and pushes the door open, jumping at me like a crazy person would. She hugs me so hard it stings. It doesn't hurt as much as the instant expansion of my heart. We tremble and shake, clinging to each other. She mutters things I don't comprehend, and I die a little inside, realizing how much she has aged. I have aged her. She feels frail in my arms, and I know that's not the truth of it. She was strong once. Strong for me. I may not remember anything, but I know that. It's just a fact that sits inside me, like the sky is blue and the grass is green. My aunt Pat was strong for me.

She pulls me back, shaking her head. "They said—"

"I know. It doesn't matter."

Anger replaces the worry and excitement on her face. "Where was you?" she asks in her thick Alabama accent, but more bitterly than I recall it being—like I might have controlled the circumstances in which I have been gone.

I swallow hard. "Injured in an accident. I don't remember anything from before. Everyone thought I was dead."

She sniffles, gasping for air as slight whimpers leave her parted lips. The dramatic cry she isn't releasing seems stuck in her throat, lodged. We hug again, just standing on the porch, attached to each other. Finally, she pulls me inside, closing the door. "How far does your memory go back?"

"Three years."

She winces. "How do you remember me?"

"You're all I remember."

A smile crosses her thin lips, spreading the crease lines from her cigarettes. She sits, lighting up a smoke. "Sit; ignore the mess. I want to know everything."

I sit across from her on the smoke-coated floral couch and nod. "There isn't much. I've been in Seattle. I didn't know I wasn't from the West Coast all this time." I sigh, finding my strength. "I need to know some things about me, from before."

Her eyes narrow. I can see her not wanting to go back there. "There ain't nothing in the past worth finding, my love."

My love.

My love was her pet name for me.

"I still need to know. Even the bad stuff."

She butts the smoke out and leans forward. "He's dead, so it don't matter none now anyway."

"How did he die?"

"He took a stroke. It was real slow, they figure. Paralyzed in his house, slowly dying of thirst and hunger and eventually fading away." Her fierceness weakens, but there is a grim smile on her face when she speaks. The story burns inside us both, but I still need to know it. "When your father was found, his cats had—well, it was real nasty."

I don't know if I have words for something so horrific. He died slowly and in agony over the course of days and then was eaten by his cats. Did they even wait for him to die? I remember reading something that said they wouldn't even wait—if given the chance, they'd eat you now. She seems content in the knowledge too. Obviously, that's creepy.

She stirs in her seat. "How have you been?"

I shake my head. "I hardly know. I've been lost, I guess, so not so good. But my life was great. I worked in a little shop and dated a loving man. I had a best friend and a cat. It was good." I still want it back.

She looks wounded. "That's real nice, I guess."

"The minute I found out who I was, I came here."

"I'm glad you came. It's been real hard thinking you was dead."

I hate that she has lived through this, especially since she is the person who was my savior when I needed her.

"Are you okay for money?" I ask it, not certain if we are close that way or not. But I have some savings.

She smiles wide. "I got a letter when you was declared dead. It had a check for compensation. I couldn't even spend the money in this lifetime if I tried." She pauses, blushing. "Lord, I s'pose I'll have to give the money back now."

I shake my head. "No. They won't make you pay it back. You earned it with pain and suffering."

She grins. "Well then, yeah. I'm just dandy." Her bitter grin fades into a real one. "Better now that you're here. Can you stay long?"

"Not this time, but I'll be back, I promise." I lift my finger, pointing at the door. "There's a man from the government waiting for me outside. I just had to come and see you. It's part of my treatment to get my memory back."

A worried look joins the wrinkles on her face. "You still working for them?"

I nod slowly. It's a lie, but it might help her sleep better to know I have a job. "They're just trying something to jog my memories. My father is a trigger for me, apparently. I just need a few details."

Her brow furrows, but she stands hesitantly, leaving the room without speaking. She's gone for several minutes, leaving me alone in the room. My eyes start to wander, taking a trip across the walls of the small front room. Pictures of me, my aunt, and the cat line the walls. My school pictures start young: ten, I'd say—maybe even younger. They go to university and military. The three of us are one tiny happy family in the group shots.

There are very few pictures of me with my mom before she died, and none with my father. As far as these walls tell, he never existed.

She clears her throat when she comes back in holding a file folder. She grips it in a way that has me convinced she doesn't mean to give it to me. But she holds it out with a trembling hand. "I will not discuss it, but I think some answers are in here." She takes my hand in hers when I stand and reach for it. Her blue eyes fill with emotion as she speaks gravely. "Leave this in the past, Sam. This doesn't belong to you anymore. It never was yours; it was always his."

I nod, letting her wrap her frail arms around me once more. When I close my eyes and inhale her, I swear I'm back to being a kid. "I missed you so much," she says.

"Me too. I didn't know what it was, but the hole in my heart feels so much smaller with you here."

Her voice sounds wet when she mutters into my neck, "Don't stay away so long this time."

"I won't. I'll be back before you know it." I hold her, trying to convince myself of the reasons I could stay here with her. I haven't felt like I was at home in ages, and in this home I do.

She kisses me on the cheek. "Can you stay one night?"

I nod. "I'll go tell the man with me to come back for me tomorrow."

"You can sleep in your old bed. It'll be like before you left for college."

I sigh into her, agreeing and anticipating sleeping in my old bed and being away from all of this for one night. I slip from her arms and head for the front door. I open it, waving at Rory. He climbs from the car, cocking an eyebrow.

"Get a hotel; I'm staying with my aunt tonight."

"Seriously? You couldn't have told me that half an hour ago?"

I lift my middle finger up out of my pocket. "Here's my apology." It's the crudest thing I've ever done, that I recall.

He grins as if he expected nothing less.

I turn back inside, closing the door and leaning my back against it.

"I can make falafels. They were your favorite when you were little. No meat, ever."

I nod, not bothering to tell her I eat meat just fine now. Her excited smile and lit-up eyes are the best image I have seen in a long time.

When I go to bed that night, I am at perfect peace. My eyes are heavy, too heavy to read the file folder. I fear there is terrible stuff that will ruin my sleep, so I leave it, not wanting to ruin the perfect day. My room looks like maybe it hasn't changed since I left, a very long time ago. There are posters of people I don't recall, and figurines. The bedspread looks old, and yet it's softer than any I have slept on. The window overlooks the yard next door, with a large tree between the two houses.

I climb into the small bed, noticing the lack of comfort but recalling it in some way. I fall asleep quickly, dreaming about Binx and Derek and a plate filled with spaghetti.

My sleep is restless, and at one point I lift my head, unsure of where I am. There is a shadow of a man standing in the corner. I blink, unsure of his actually being there or not. I part my lips to scream when I realize there truly is a shadow cast by a man.

Derek steps into the dim light of the alarm clock, putting his finger to his lips.

I don't move. It's similar to being hunted by a lion or a panther. Seeing him in the shadows makes me lean more toward panther. His eyes are filled with all kinds of crazy. When he sees I'm not going to scream he relaxes, still keeping his finger to his lips.

The look on his face grows soft and peaceful. My eyes fuzz out, but the image of him smiling at me from the shadows gets stuck in my head. I feel things, like his hands holding me and air whooshing around my body. Wind and heavy air hit my face as I jerk as if going downward.

My eyes open as my head drops back and I see the family photos, but they're upside down. His breath hits me in the face as he takes each stair to the main floor. My eyes flutter, and I lose a second.

Suddenly the room feels different as everything spins and cool thick air drags its way across my body. I lose everything there, all sense and consciousness.

When I wake I'm in the back of a moving car. Derek is driving. Seeing him makes me smile, but something feels wrong. Waking is still a foggy mess for me. I don't remember why we got into the car. I don't remember why we aren't in the Mercedes.

My head spins, and I have to replay the last couple of memories to figure out that I shouldn't be in any car with him. It's hard when he's the only thing I recall for years. I instantly trust him every time I see him.

He glances back at me, smiling. It isn't the one I love. It's not a full smile—his heart's not in it. "You're awake."

"What are you doing?" I almost want to ask what he's going to do to me, but I think starting off accusing him of things is a bad plan. I don't know what makes him snap. He's always been sweet to me. I haven't ever seen him lose his mind.

He lifts the folder from my room. "Do you know the effort it took to make this go away? Do you know how hard it was for me to take this from you? Why can't you see that this was the whole reason for it all?"

My heart stops. "What's in that folder?"

His expression changes. "I'm going to show you."

I sit up, rubbing my eyes and trying not to vomit. "What did you give me?"

"Your sedative." His eyes find me in the rearview. "I have tried to protect you from yourself for years, Jane. Years. Everything is for you. If you say you'll trust me and won't fight me on this, we can turn around and drive to a new place. We won't have to discuss this anymore." He pleads with his eyes.

I shake my head. "I need to know. I need you to tell me what's going on."

A defeated look crosses his eyes. He doesn't talk again. I curl up in the backseat, contemplating what chance I have of escaping. It doesn't look good. I'm lethargic from the sedative and not nearly as strong as he is.

When he stops the car I realize my eyes are closed; like an idiot I've relaxed. It's hard not to. He makes me calm. He's still the person in the world I trust the most.

I stretch, looking around. Instantly I'm panicked. We are parked outside of a small house. My father's house.

My heart starts first, followed by my mouth drying out and my eyes watering. He sighs, staring at the house. "Don't make me do this," he mutters.

"Okay. I trust you. I don't want to go in there. I'll do whatever you want, just don't make me go in there."

"Don't lie to me, Jane. I know you far better than you know your-self." He doesn't look back, but I can hear the emotion in his voice. "You're making me do this because you don't believe I have your best interests at heart." He takes a few deep breaths. Each one echoes in the silence of the car, torturing me with its intensity. When he's worked himself up enough, he gets out abruptly, ripping open the door.

"Don't do this. I don't want to do this. Let me come with you. I'll be good. I'll stay with you forever."

When his hands come for me I fight and scream, but the difference in us is remarkable. He drags me, kicking and screaming, from the car. I know I make contact with my flailing legs and arms but he doesn't flinch. I scratch and bite but his hands are strong, nearly as strong as his will. He flips me over his shoulders, carrying me inside. He kicks the door open, letting light into the dank space. When he gets inside the small front room, he closes the door. I scream again, but he lowers me, clamping a hand over my face. "Shhhhh. You don't want to disturb the energy here. Let it lie; it's better when it's calm in here."

I don't know what he's talking about. I don't even care. I just want out. My insides feel like a bomb has gone off. He holds my back to his chest with his arms wrapped around me, making me face the room like I am facing a fear of the dark or monsters.

He leans his mouth down close to my cheek, speaking in my ear with breathy whispers: "When I met you, you had to sleep with the night-light on. You were the only agent I knew of who went days without sleep because of it. The dark scared you." He's trembling, but he doesn't stop. He walks us farther into the house, pushing me forward with his body. "This living room is where he usually got you to do things for the camera. He filmed it."

The word *diddle* suddenly burns in my head. I gag on his hand, losing my fight as all will and strength is sucked from me. I flop onto my knees as images of the camera flicker in my fuzzy memories with jerks. Words float into my head, words and images. A sweaty fat man talks slowly, talking about how he wants things done. Hot tears fill my eyes. They're desperate to block it all out. They want this to end. They don't want me to see. But the problem is the things I see are inside me. My tears can't block them out.

"Your aunt's file was mostly from after the police got involved. It's essentially the police report she was shown. I have added the pictures you had from before the police got involved. The ones you made me keep, even though they have burned a hole in my heart just by existing." His voice shakes.

I hear the rustling of papers as a heavy sickness covers me like a cloud of very bad things. They've waited for me to come back. The cloud sat on the ceiling, building and gathering strength so when I came here it could rain down on me. I open my eyes, realizing I have been watching a movie in my head. The papers from the folder are spread across the wooden floor, snapshots of the evil inside me. The vileness of my soul has been captured on film. They capture a young girl doing things she shouldn't know how to do. Hands and faces, body parts I refuse to see. I can't see her face or her tears. I refuse to see her.

Horrors of the worst kind sit there, taunting me with the possibility I remember all of this but have repressed it.

Derek takes my hand, forcing me to stand, and pulls me into the hallway. Every inch of my body clamps and tightens, squeezing and crying out for our feet to freeze. The hot tears won't stop, and my mouth won't open. It's clamped in protest. He opens a door at the end of the hall. Muted light floods through dirty windows, making shadows on the wooden floors. Shadows that become monsters, or rather feed the ones that are already here, lurking.

I know this room.

I know this evil.

"This was your room. I made sure everything ended here for him. It was the only way. He needed to go in the worst way possible, but I wanted to make sure he went here."

The room is bare, but I can still see it all. I can still see the small wooden bed and the little plastic bin for my clothes that was shaped like a dresser but not one. A poor child's dresser. My father always said it was an upgrade from a box. My eyes dart to the closet where the other bin was, the secret bin. I was never allowed to touch that bin. It was for the shows. They were the only things that made him happy. He never hit or hurt me when I did the shows in the pretty clothes.

I back up slowly, feeling my stomach gurgling. I turn, running from the room. I leap out the front door, losing my stomach onto the gravel and weeds. I heave until there's nothing but tears leaving my eyes next to the ropes of spit and drool.

Derek's hands are there suddenly, holding me. My soft whimpers become sobbing. I don't know how to get past this moment. It feels like a cage that has been lowered over top of me, trapping me back where I once was, stuck in my head.

My heart is burning and my stomach aching, but even worse is the way my blinding tears make a mess of the view I have of the world. They make it pretty with a kaleidoscope of shapes and colors. He rubs my back, and I now see how far he would go to love me and protect me and save me. I finally understand his obsession with my memory and the bad things I have saddled him with. I don't know why I did it. I don't know why I made him know those things and let myself forget.

But I know why I forgot.

I wish I could again.

There is a horror show inside me. A lifetime of misery that was squeezed into a few short years and made to be enough to ruin me forever.

"Just breathe, Jane. Deep breaths will calm you down."

I shake my head. "I remember. Pat came to the house when the police called her. She fought with them in the yard, arguing about what they were going to do about it all. They left, and she took me. She smoked and sang, and everything changed from that moment on. He never saw me again. She made sure. I was nine."

He rubs like he's massaging. "She saved you, but she couldn't save all of you. The memories and the nightmares and the sleepwalking. It was all mental scarring, damage that couldn't be healed."

The sleepwalking still seems crazy, but the small house of horrors seems crazier. The fact that's all that's wrong with me is a miracle. The memories weigh a ton inside me, and I know I have only a tenth of what's there.

He lifts me up, carrying me back to the car. He places me inside, laying me down. I curl into the fetal position, holding myself tightly. "Who knows about this?"

"Everyone. Your personnel file has it mentioned a few times."

I glance up at him. He's on his knees in the dirt, staring at me. He looks apprehensive and scared. "So the world knew he was doing those things and they never took me away?"

"They put you in a home for foster kids because Pat was your only living relative. Pat lost it. She wanted to be certain you were not going into a home where the same thing would happen to you. She wanted to bring you to Texas, where she was living for work, but they said that you couldn't leave the state until after the trial, and she had to apply for adoption. She knew the process would be lengthy, and you were a mess, so she just took you. She went the opposite way to North Carolina and rented a house and got a job and never looked back. She put you in therapy, but it didn't help, and you ended up repressing most of it, recalling only a few details. But in your sleep it all comes back and you sleepwalk, kill things, and act savage. You have always done it. When you joined the military and government they used your lack of emotion for their benefit. The same way they did me." He strokes my head soothingly. "When we were assigned each other, we found one another in the dark, Jane, but we made light for one another. You are my light and I am yours."

I believe him, but I fear I will always be stuck in the things that are associated with this house. I won't age or grow beyond those moments. They're a roadblock in my mind and heart.

10. SEE SAM LIE

The ride across town is painful. I don't know what to think or say. Every thought has become linked to some aspect of the secrets I now know, secrets I gave up everything to forget. "I need to see Pat."

He looks back at me with a frown. "We are disappearing, Jane. We need to re-create ourselves again. I'm taking this away from you again, erasing the damage. You understand why, right?"

"Yeah, but I don't want to leave her hanging like that again."

He sighs but nods. "You can say good-bye this time. But then we leave and forget all about this vile coastline. There is nothing but horridness here. We'll go to Europe, enjoy a beach or a village where nothing bad will ever happen."

I nod. I'm lost on what else to do. He's right, even if I don't want brain surgery again. I'm not fond of the idea of being back where I started when my memory was erased, but I want the filthy feelings inside me gone, forever. I never want to come back here or see any of this again. I close my eyes, putting the passenger seat in recline. "How did we decide on the plan? The one where you erase my memories."

"It wasn't the plan at first."

"Just tell me how it happened."

"It's a long story." He sounds like he's trying to dissuade me from being interested.

"It's a long drive back to North Carolina."

His voice calms considerably, regardless of the disturbing aspects to the story. "I decided to kill you. I decided that it didn't matter that I loved you. It was you or me, and I was choosing me. I got to your house, snuck inside, made a sandwich, and watched you sleep. I turned the night-light off, not fully understanding the ramifications that would have. I was halfway through my sandwich when you started to whimper. I don't know why, but I walked to you, touching your hand so you would fall back to sleep. But you were awake, or so I thought. You reached over to undo my pants, tears running down your cheeks. I realized then how damaged you were. It broke my heart, what was left of it." He turns, facing me, and I can see the raw emotions playing upon his face. "I understood the pain you harbored and the suffering you had endured. So I woke you from the strange sleepwalking sex act you were about to commit. We fought, wrestled around the room, you trying to kill me and me trying to defend myself without killing you. Eventually, I overpowered you and told you I knew who you were but I loved you. We kissed." He stops there, but he's blushing like there's more to the story.

"Then what happened?"

He shrugs. "Well, nothing. Don't get me wrong—you wanted more, but I could see what it all meant to you. Sex was a way to manipulate men and control them. So we talked. I came over every night. We talked and I cooked, and then we talked some more until one night you fell asleep with the lights off. When you woke in the morning we stayed in the bed, in the silence, and we knew. I confessed I didn't want to kill you, and I didn't want to die, so the only solution was to run."

"And that's where we are now? On the run again?"

His eyes narrow as if he's squinting to look down the highway better. "Not exactly." He sighs. "We burned the car after the accident we staged and tried for three years to be an honest couple, traveling and hiding from our employers. But you slowly got worse and worse. Your paranoia, nightmares, and sleepwalking were getting so bad I didn't know what else to do. The job had been a focus for you. It had closed off your brain. When you worked you didn't have nightmares or sleepwalk. I looked into people with amnesia, operations that caused it, and accidents that resulted in it. We decided together it was the best option for you." He pulls over to the side of the road and gets out of the car. He messes around in the trunk and comes back with a small box. He hands it to me and drives on. "This is everything we had from before the operation."

He drives, and I flip through three years of my life that I will never get back. There is a small photo album with trips to different countries and holidays. In the beginning we are smiling and look happy. As I flip through it I can see the decline in myself. My skin becomes sallow and pale. My eyes have huge bags under them. My hair is darker and darker but messier and less glossy. By the end, in every photo I can see worry in his eyes and a hollow distant stare in mine. The last three pages are photos of me sleeping on trains and in cars and in beds. It's disturbing how easily my father chased us around the world, even after he was dead.

When we get back to Pat's, he stops the car, giving me a look. "Five minutes, okay?"

I nod, getting out and carrying the album to the front door. She opens the door with a leery look on her face. "You was gone when I got up. Ya been gone the whole day. I thought we was gonna spend time together."

I nod. "Sorry. I had to see something." She glances past me to the man in the car. I lift the photo album to block her view. "I have something I need you to see and that I need you to know." She looks confused but opens the door wider so we can both walk in. I sit down on the floral couch and brace myself for the very real possibility she is going to tell me I am insane.

I flip to the start of the book. "Six years ago I ran away with a man named Benjamin. He was the first person I think I ever loved."

She scowls at the photos. "I never heard of him."

"I kept him secret. We traveled for three years, and I spent every waking moment trying to outrun my father and the things he did after Mom died."

She swallows hard, shuddering a little. I know that feeling well.

"I went everywhere and did everything I could to be rid of it all, but it didn't work." I flip pages until I get to the depressed pages. She points at the one of me looking particularly horrid. "That's how your momma looked when she died."

I nod, not even a little suspicious about how that happened. "Well, I was done. I needed a new life. So I had an operation to make me forget everything. When I woke, I was told I was in an accident. I was told I was a victim of amnesia. I was convinced my life was perfect before the car accident. I had a great man who cared for me and a cat named Binx."

The name of the cat makes her cry as she nods. "That makes sense."

I turn to her as tears start to roll down my cheeks. "I need to go back to that place. That beautiful oblivion that sits there waiting for me. The innocence of my mind and creation of my new past is the only thing that's going to save me."

Tears roll from her oddly colored eyes, looking similar to mine, I imagine. She sniffles, sucking her trembling breaths momentarily before nodding again. "I don't blame you at all. If I could have taken it all away I woulda. I woulda done anything. I woulda walked through fire to make it go away. I didn't know what was happening until the school called the social workers for help. I just didn't know." She lifts my hand to her lips and kisses, closing her eyes and gripping me. "Is there a world where I won't remind you of him, or do I have to stay here in this world?"

I nod. "I think so. But you gotta leave this all behind. You must come with us, not tell anyone where you're going and not be in communication with anyone. Can you do that?"

"I can."

I wrap my arms around her, gripping her. "You are going to have to trust Benjamin Dash. Whatever he says is how it goes. He knows how to do this. He's the person I trusted last time with my memory erasing."

She sniffles and smiles, leaning into me more. "I will do whatever it takes. I don't want to lose you again, Sam."

The name makes me feel dirty. "Jane. I like Jane."

"Jane it is."

"We're going to bring you with us this time. Pack your things, Aunty. You won't be able to bring much, just the basics." I kiss her cheek and get up, leaving her there. When I look back I try to be as upbeat as I can. "I'll send him to come and get you. He uses the name Derek since we ran away."

She smiles nicely. "I'll be ready when he comes."

"I have to go. The government might be watching the house." I wave, clutching my photo album and hurrying outside. I run down the stairs to the car, realizing I might have led Derek into a trap.

When I get into the car he cocks a dark eyebrow at me. "Something you want to tell me?"

I nod. "Two things. She's coming with me this time, and we have to leave now. Rory might be watching the house."

He lifts his thumb, pointing behind us. "He's right there." He starts the car, driving carefully until he rounds the corner, and then lets his driving loose. He skids around the next corner, flying through the residential area, using the parking brake to skid around the next corner into an alley. We have done a complete rectangle, only we exit out the back of the neighborhood, away from my house. He drives fast, speeding away. I'm nervous, but he looks pissed so I don't say anything about the driving. Instead, my hands don't leave the holy-shit handles, and my breath doesn't leave my lungs.

He turns several corners, passing people on the wrong side. Eventually, I close my eyes, ready to flip out. In the dark of my closed eyes, the driving feels more like a topsy-turvy sea, tossing our boat about. Suddenly we come to a complete stop, back up abruptly, and stop again. He turns the car off and sits quietly with only his breath making noises.

I open an eye, scared of what I'll find, but it's actually quite beautiful. He's driven us to a small house with a huge yard surrounded by tall trees. The manicured spot is stunning—the sort of yard you would imagine grandparents would have out of boredom. No working person could maintain something like this. Rosebushes line the bases of the trees on one side and lilac bushes the other side. It must be fragrant in the spring and summer. We are parked in a garage of sorts next to the little white house. My hands cramp up as I release them from the handle, giving him a confused look. "Did you lose them?"

He nods. "Why did you trust him, of all people?" His voice is cold and distant. I don't recognize it. "Why him?"

"He had a lot of evidence against you, and none of it proved you worked for any agency. You look like a serial killer to them."

A small smile toys with his luscious lips. "I am what I am, Jane. I just prefer not to classify it."

Something about the statement chills me. I know he's sick. I can see it on him when he loses his control, but it's easy to forget about when he's being the Derek I've always known. It's easy to see him as a regular man. To me he is the only man. I take his hand in mine, trying to ignore how cool and clammy it is when I bring it to my lips. "I love you, Derek."

He shakes his head. "I know you love me, but you don't know me, Jane. Not really."

"I do know you. I remember knowing you and loving you. But I prefer the Derek you were in Seattle."

His gray eyes are void of all green. I think that the green is the goodness in him and the gray is the evil. When he's too full up on bad, the green doesn't show. I lean forward, completely terrified of the man I am pressing my lips against, and yet intrigued that he is the gentle giant with me. He never hurts me. I don't think he can.

He kisses back. It's wooden and unemotional, but it warms slowly. His lips begin to move, rubbing against mine. Our fingers find their way up each other's arms, gripping each other.

The car is like a trap, preventing us from moving much beyond the caressing and kissing, but I can tell we both feel the need to move. He lets go of me, jumping out of the car and rushing to my side. His footsteps on the gravel beneath us are intense. When he drags me from the car it's rough, but I fight a moan over the violence of our sudden outburst. He pushes me to the hood of the car, bending me across it, face down and writhing. My pants are ripped down, baring my ass to the garden. I hear him spit. It makes me cringe until he pushes his erection inside me, bringing instant pleasure with it. Then I ignore the way it got there. He thrusts hard, sliding his hands up my back and into my hair. He drags my head back, lifting my upper body. His other hand slides across the front of me and into the top of my shirt. He dips his entire hand into my bra, rolling my nipple as he drives his cock forward, bumping my thighs and hips off the hood and bumper.

It is not love we make. His fingers grab too hard, his cock enters too roughly, and when his teeth find my back I cry out. But none of my responses are in pain or injury. When I orgasm he can hardly move with the tension inside me gripping him. But the second I'm done quivering all over his erection, he's back to jackhammering me into the car. He pushes my face back down, sliding my cheek and lips up and down the gray car. Words leave my mouth, words I don't comprehend at all. They're mutterings to my ears but to my brain they're the true sound of bliss.

When he's about to come, he grips my ass cheeks hard, pulling me back onto him as his balls slap against me.

I cry out again, shocked by the eruption inside me—a second orgasm. I don't suspect it's coming, but the moment it hits he loses himself, coming at the same time. His orgasm drips from us both as he collapses on top of me, pushing me into the metal hood harder.

"God damn, I missed you, Sam." He kisses my back, and instantly I am unsure how turned on I should be by the events that have transpired in a stranger's yard.

Sam?

I don't know the appropriate response to the name, and my trembling vagina isn't going to be any help on the matter. She's convinced we need him, forever.

11. SEE JANE DIE

There is no way to go back when we enter the airport. The passport in my hand is a lie. The place we are going to do the surgery is a mystery. The act we are about to commit is a crime.

"She's coming, right?" I ask, scanning the area for the one face I need to see in the crowd.

He kisses the back of my hand, an act from before the truth came out. It is an act old Derek would have done, not the man he's been since my father's house. I have moaned through that version of Derek's affection several times in the last twenty-four hours. "I told you she is, three times already. Stop asking, Jane."

And we are back to Jane? Maybe he's back to being old Derek.

I don't understand so I don't pry. I don't know where to go with all of it. The emotions and confusion have taken up enough room inside me. I decided to trust him when I saw the house of horrors, and I'm not changing my mind. Course I said I'd never trust him once I saw the video old me made. Maybe making guarantees is a bad plan for me.

All I know is every time I close my eyes I'm back there, and I need it gone—need my father gone. I need to be free of all of this. Derek is the only person who has ever made me free. It was a short freedom, ending after only three years, but it was the happiest I have ever been since before my mother died. I know that as a truth inside me.

"No more sleeping with the light on as of Wednesday." He kisses my hand again.

I nod, hating the fact I have completely reverted back to the sleepwalking, assaulting him sexually in his sleep, all the while crying and whimpering, and needing the light on. It's disturbing me.

We walk past the airline counters toward the security area. When I see her my heart lights up. I don't wave or smile, I just glow on the inside.

She acts as though she doesn't know us and walks to the bathroom. I want to scratch my wig and adjust it but I don't. The bright-blonde hair is my only chance at getting onto the plane. I leave his side, walking to the bathroom with her passport in hand. She knows to go to the American Airlines gate and ask for the ticket that's been left there for her, the new her. When I get in the bathroom she hugs me, breathing as if she hasn't since I left her house. "Thank the gods you're all right."

I pull back. "Why?"

She shakes her wrinkled face. "There was a man, the one who was at the house with you the first day. He brought me this, this morning. He said he needed you to have it and that it was the same as last time." She hands me a scratched-up pale-pink phone. I scowl, taking it.

"Did they follow you?"

She shakes her head. "No. I took a bus, a cab, and then walked through an older area before catching another cab. It would have been impossible. I brought nothing with me but what is in this carry-on."

"Okay." I hand her the passport. "You're a Canadian named Martha Jane Anderson. You're from Toronto and were here to see an old friend, but now you're leaving on vacation. Make sure you memorize the address and stuff."

"I can do that." She nods. "See you wherever we end up, I guess."

It makes me grin, knowing she's coming this time. I'll have someone who's mine. I wish I could bring Angie. I hate that I'm leaving her behind. She and Binx are my family too. I already miss them both, even though it's only been days. I can't wait to get Binx back. His stay in the kennel is going to make him extra cranky. I almost grin, thinking about how sassy he's going to be.

My aunt kisses me once more before leaving the bathroom and heading for the airline counter. Once I'm alone the weight of the phone feels like the gun he gave me did.

I press the power button on, knowing full well he's tracked my aunt here. I dial 911 and wait for it to ring.

"Why are you trying to make me crazy? This isn't even funny, Sam," Rory answers, sounding desperate. "We are moving in to bring him down. We need you to stand down on this one. Please, for me."

I close my eyes, letting the things I need to fall from my lips. "If you ever cared about me, even a little, I need you to imagine your father made you do the things mine did. Imagine for two seconds how you would feel knowing you woke in the night and killed animals like you once saw your father do." He tries to interrupt me but I keep going. "Imagine for one minute how it feels to know someone took everything from you and left you a shell. How would you manage all of that baggage?"

"Don't do this. Whatever his plan is, don't do it."

"I want this to go away. I need to be free of it all."

His voice cracks. "Don't leave me again."

I shake my head as if he can see me. "I want you to go away, and I never want to see you again."

"He isn't the person you think he is. Trust me, you had to have had a plan. There's no way you let him brainwash you without there being a method to your madness."

A heavy sigh leaves my lips with my next sentence. "Let me be dead, Rory. Let me just be dead. This is me begging you to let me be free of this. Don't be the person who traps me in the world my father tortured me in." I hang up the phone, leaving it in the garbage can, and walk from the bathroom. My eyes are filled with tears, but my mind is certain we are doing the right thing.

I walk back to Derek, trying to hide the fact I've been crying, but he sees it immediately. "You all right?"

I nod. "Just a little sad still. My heart hurts, ya know?"

He wraps an arm around me. "I do." We walk to the security check. It's there I discover we are headed to Austria, which makes me excited. I know I've been there before. I saw the pictures, but I don't recall it.

We walk to the gate for the plane, sitting next to each other on a bench. Earlier I told him I thought coming to the airport and taking the same flight was a gamble, but he said he picked the flight for a reason—it was overbooked.

He kisses my hand again, muttering, "I'll be right back."

I nod, waiting for him. Everything is clicking into place. I watch him walk down the long corridor of tan carpet, past the gates of the departure area. He's crazy, there's no doubt, but he wouldn't ever hurt me. I know that. He's the only way I'll ever be rid of the haunting details of my childhood. I wish he could just take away the last two weeks but leave me with everything else. I was never scared before, except when I worried he would eventually see what a plain Jane I was. *Plain Jane.* The words ring in my head. *Plain Jane.*

I open my mouth, whispering the words, "Plain Jane."

It acts likes a trigger. A darkness covers my face, like a bucket of blood has been poured over my head, making my vision turn red and cloud out my view. My eyes flutter like I'm having a seizure, only I'm not making them do it. A thousand images wash through my head at once, like a flood filling my brain.

Memories clear away, leaving one distinct image in my mind. I see him, my father. He's on a bed, tied there. He's old—older than my other memories of him. I'm in the room, smiling wide at him as I inject a needle into his fat hairy arm. He cries out in pain, making me jerk the needle a little more. I can see it dragging under the skin as he screams. There's a small second when I almost open my eyes to stop the image, but I don't. I force myself to watch as I drag a blade across his chest, cutting in. Then I pour a type of acid across the skin. In the haze I see the label of the white bottle as my gloved hand lifts it—citric acid. His screams are delicious. I rub him down with cream, his entire naked body including his flaccid cock; touching it makes me gag but I do it. I douse him in something that makes him scream in a way that just seeing the memory makes me shudder. His skin is flaming red, and his eyes are bulging from his fat head. He goes pale in the face after a few moments, clearly in shock. I grab the paddles and shock him to bring him back.

He screams and cries. He begs and pleads. But like my words once fell on his deaf ears, his do now to mine.

The scene fades away. I open my eyes, unsure how Derek could have killed my father if I was the one torturing him.

The airport isn't any different when my eyelids lift, but I am.

I remember small bits of being me. It's not whole, but the bits and pieces give me a clue to a few things I didn't know.

I remember Rory—I remember not hating him at all.

Getting up, I hurry down the hall to the bathroom. The door slams open as I burst through it and instantly stick my arm into the trash bin. My fingers touch things I might have squealed about seconds ago, but now I'm unfazed by it. My armpit pinches as I reach to the very bottom of the trash and paper until I touch the pale-pink phone. I squeeze it with my fingertips, lifting it slowly so I don't drop it back into the filth. I press 911 and put it on speakerphone, not even washing my hands.

"Tell me you changed your mind." Rory's desperate voice makes me wince.

"Ror, I need you." He doesn't respond, so I speak again. "Ror? You there?"

I can hear him breathing and, I swear, swallowing hard. "Sam?"

I wince again. The name is mine. "Yeah. It's me."

"You remember?"

"Sort of." I nod, like he can see me doing it. "I think so. I think I remember a lot of things. I need you to come and get me. My aunt was at the American Airlines counter and got a ticket to Austria. I need her found and taken somewhere safe."

Again he pauses. "We followed her to the gate for Colorado, not Austria. She's there now. I was just looking at her. We got here about ten minutes ago. She was being incredibly slippery earlier. We tracked the phone and followed that way. We assumed she meant to leave the phone at the airport and sneak out another way. That's sort of the thing Dash would do."

It's my turn to pause. "Fuck. He might actually be doing that. He left me at the gate for Austria. What if he ran?"

"Come to the Colorado gate. It's twenty-seven. Come here and we'll regroup."

"Okay." I don't want to leave Derek/Dash in case he's on to me. I don't want him to run. I have to assume I've wasted almost seven years trying to get him. "I'll be there in a couple of minutes." My head isn't clear, and my heart is conflicted, but my thirst for revenge has become the only emotion I am capable of feeling.

He didn't kill my father.

He didn't save me.

I saved myself.

Fuck him. Guess I am back to not trusting him again. The back-and-forth is making me dizzy.

Before I go, I scrub my hands thoroughly to wash off the trash-bin filth. When I've dried my hands twice, I leave, constantly scanning the hall for him. In the seats for the gate to Austria I see him. His head cocks to the side, he lifts an eyebrow, and stands, walking toward me. He stops ten feet from me. "Plain Jane find her way home?"

The sentence makes me tremble. "What did you do to me?"

"I couldn't kill you, Sam. I know I should have. I know I should have killed you and been done with it, but I couldn't. And you wouldn't listen, would you? You never do."

"Oh God, you did this to me twice, didn't you? This is the second time you've screwed with my brain. I've remembered already once, haven't I? What was it that time?"

"We were in California, and there was something like the Ronald problem." He shrugs, and I hate him. It's less than I love him, but it's enough to keep me from walking to him.

"You killed Ronald?" The answer is so obvious now. I suspect I always knew that. He smiles wide, making my hate grow. "You killed Ronald? Why are you doing this?" It's the only question I have.

"Jane, I need you to understand that for me this isn't over." His sickening smile sells me on the severity of his disease, past the fog in my head and the way I make myself see him. For the first time I really and truly see the man behind the curtain. He nods. "It won't ever be. You can run and you can hide, and I will chase you because we are meant to be. We are each other's light."

I follow his advice, turning and running as fast as I can. I don't know what else to do.

12. WHAT WHIP MARKS?

When I get to the gate for Colorado I pause. I recognize Antoine and Rory at once, but the woman they're sitting by isn't my aunt. She looks similar, but she is definitely not my aunt. I frown, bringing Rory to me with just the look. He smiles cautiously. "Hey!"

I look at the woman. "That's not my aunt."

He glances at her. "I know that."

"Where's my aunt?"

"In custody. She thinks you're in danger, and she's freaking out." He looks past me. "Where's Dash?"

I point behind me with my thumb. "Back there. He's freaking out too. Mostly just freaking me out." I look up into Rory's dark-blue eyes and nod. "I need some answers from you—now. No holding back."

"What do ya remember?"

"Not much." I shake my head, not sure how to tell him what I do remember. But the crowded and noisy airport suddenly seems like the perfect place to blurt out something so horrid. If I'm lucky the words will get lost in the noise and crowds of this hectic place. I need to say it aloud to rid myself of the burden of being the only one who knows, and he suddenly seems like the right person to tell. Taking a large breath, I prepare myself for the sentence as I say it. "I think I might have kil—murdered my father and hidden it like it was an accident."

He glances at me in a funny way, clearly disbelieving my statement. "We were in Germany when your dad died. I know, because I was with ya when you got the call."

"I remember torturing him. I burned him and cut him and made him scream."

"Well, not to sound like you're insane and remembering shit that never happened, but if the cuckoo shoe fits, ya might have to wear it." He lifts a cynical eyebrow, and the disbelief thickens in his tone. "You couldn't be in the same room as your dad, no matter what. I also know this for a fact because I was with you once when he showed up at Pat's house. You started shaking and lost all the color in your face. Pat screamed at him and called the cops. He was calling ya a liar and screaming crazy things. I didn't even know who he was until afterward, but during his two-minute stay at the front door, you became a different person."

I know we dated or something, so I ask a question he might know the answer to. "Did I have nightmares? Did I do horrible things at night? Wake with blood on me and such?"

Rory sighs. "No. What is this?"

"I don't know." And God help me, but I don't. I don't understand how any of this is possible. I have woken with blood on my hands. I recall horrible things even if they seem very unlikely. "What was I like?"

He leans on the back of a chair next to us. I don't know if he's contemplating telling me the truth or if he's trying to find the words. Either way, I have to assume it's bad. "Sarcastic and bitchy. Sort of a control freak. Ya never liked anyone to help ya with anything. You'd fuck something up six times and get it right on the seventh and still not take a hand from someone who knew how to do it. Ya drove me nuttier than squirrel shit. Ya slept with a night-light. That was odd and annoying to the people in the room who liked it dark." His smile twists into a wry grin. "But ya were worth every second spent sleeping in a lit room."

I sigh. "Can you try to be professional?"

"No, but I'll be honest. Ya were a badass bitch who liked to do things her way and get fucked, hard. Ya didn't like things soft or slow. Ya didn't like men who were sweet, and ya didn't cry, ever."

I step back, sort of scared I might have actually been a man. "I never cried, not even with sad movies when animals were hurt or killed?" I don't even want to touch on the sex.

His dark-blue eyes narrow. "I'm starting to think your memory isn't back, Sam."

I nod in agreement, completely lost on the things inside me.

He links his arm in mine, pulling me down the long corridor to the security checkpoint. "Let's get out of here before ya go and start telling me how bad your period was last month."

I glare at him. "I don't get periods, ass."

He pauses. "What? Ya were a right bitch every month—don't tell me I don't know ya."

"I haven't had a period since I can recall. Derek said I was injured in the car accident."

He purses his lips. "We need to find out what the hell is going on."

"I think we need to find out who Derek is. Or rather Benjamin or Dash or whatever his name is this week. Who he is will tell us more about what the hell happened to me." I glance into Rory's dark-blue eyes, saying the last thing I ever expected to say: "As soon as I see Pat and make sure she's all right, I want to go to my father's house." The words even make me shudder.

He gives me a sideways look but doesn't say a word. He leads me to the security desk, where Pat is sitting in a small room. When I get inside, she leaps at me, dragging the blonde wig off my head with her arm. "You're okay!"

"I am. Look, Derek turned out to be a criminal, and apparently, I might have undergone the brain surgery by force. I don't know what's happened, but I am pretty determined to find out. Until he's caught, we can't let you run around for him to abduct in order to bribe me with. Can you stay with Antoine until I know what's what?"

"Oh, uhm." Her eyes fill with worry as she glances at Antoine. She looks worried, but he offers the nicest smile I'm sure he owns. "I don't really know, my love. If he's coming after you, maybe you should just stay here with me too."

I smile, softening my face. "It's okay, I swear. I'll be safe. These guys aren't going to let anything happen to me or you."

"This isn't the first time you done said that to me, my love." Her eyes grow cold, made creepier by the different-colored anger in the different-colored eyes. She turns, directing all that freaky hate at Rory. "You better not let her get hurt or I'll kill you with my bare hands."

He swallows hard, looking nervous, but I suspect it's more like he's filtering the annoying responses he has for her threat. He nods, leaving it at that.

Antoine looks annoyed when I smile at him. "Take care of my aunt." He sighs his answer to my request and offers her his arm. "Shall we?" His face is back to being sweet again.

"Stay safe." She hugs me again before taking his arm and being led out the back doors.

Rory points after them at the doors. "We have a chopper out there. Let's use that. I don't feel like driving all the way back to Alabama."

"Flying in a helicopter?" My fear of heights whispers through me, like wind echoing through a rocky tunnel.

He grabs my arm and drags me out the back door. "Ya used to fly them, for the love of Christ and all things holy." His Irish accent thickens when he's feisty.

When we get inside he pulls on a helmet and hands me one. My fingers ache with fear and hesitation as I take it, pulling it on. I feel like maybe we should have life jackets and better padding than regular clothing. He starts the engines, putting on sunglasses and grinning at me like an idiot.

As we lift off the ground I gag, closing my eyes and waiting for the tipping feeling from the lack of ground beneath me to subside. It doesn't, so I don't open my eyes.

"You're missing everything. It's beautiful up here."

I lift a thumb into the air, not speaking or opening my eyes at all.

"Chickenshit."

I switch to my middle finger, still with my eyes closed. He chuckles, and the sound tugs at my heartstrings.

I don't know how long we fly. I honestly don't even sneak a single peek, but I am bored out of my mind when we do finally land. He shuts it off, shoving me lightly. "Wakey wakey!"

I shake my head. "Not sleeping, just counting forward and backward from a hundred repeatedly."

"You still do that?"

"Guess so." I don't open my eyes until I hear the spinny part on the top stop moving. I have a fear of having my head chopped off too.

He's standing on the grass across the yard with his arms folded when I climb out slowly. My legs tremble with each step, threatening to buckle completely. When they do, I land on my knees, gripping the grass and heaving my breath.

"What the fuck did he do to you?"

I shake my head. "Look, heights combined with a flimsy little helicopter is a completely normal fear." I gag a little bit, burping some of the bagel I had earlier as I pass gas out the back end. "I don't think my stomach is so good. We should stay here."

"No. Get up or I'll leave you here."

I wince, shudder, and fart again. At least they're silent and he's across the grass.

"Can we go? Today? Please?"

I drag myself up, wiping my hands across my face to clear the sweat. "I want to drive back."

"Not a chance." He turns and starts walking through the swampy woods. I contemplate staying, but the place makes me uncomfortable so I get up and stalk after him.

I don't even know where we are until I see the small house in the distance. This is my backyard from when I was little. As we pass a shell of what used to be a house I pause, turning toward it. It pulls me to it, capturing me in its tractor beam of magnetism. Something about this house haunts my very soul. I stop just short of the over-grown grass, looking at the collapsing walls and sunken-in roof. An image trickles through my head in flashes and flares, but not a distinct picture. "Leona Larson lived in this house." The words are mine and they aren't. I don't know how I remember it all, and yet still don't remember much. This thought is just there, like something I know. Like a fact.

I hear Rory walking on the grass, crunching on the dead yard. It's all around us. No one has cared for this house or yard in a long time. I don't think he's close, and yet I continue to speak to him. "He liked her better than me. He was nice to her. He gave her treats and made me play outside. She was supposed to babysit me, but I always had to go outside." The words join the wind in a sinister whisper. "I hated her."

"What are you doing? Do you see something?" He's so loud and in the present, but I'm stuck in the past. It's almost black-and-white—it's so old and discolored in my brain.

"He liked her better than me." My 'Bama accent is so thick I can hardly understand myself. "He gave her ice cream and told her she was real pretty."

"The Larson family?"

I turn. "You know of them?"

He looks completely confused. "Of course I do. They're the family whose eldest daughter went missing first in the area. Her family was interviewed during the whole *your dad turned out to be a monster* affair. Her father was a witness in the trial. Said he saw him beating the shit outta ya in the yard a few times and that he suspected your father in the case of his missing daughter. Nothing was ever proven."

I shake my head. "I don't remember that or what happened exactly, but I swear she was there. She was the one my father tortured."

"I think you're confused—the file says you were at school, telling one of the teachers why you didn't get your homework done." He says it like he's desperately trying to recall it all. "Yeah, you told the teacher, in great detail, I might add, about what happened to you. About how your dad was making movies so you couldn't do your homework. It was fucked up. Anyway, when your dad went to jail, the Larson family moved away. The house has been abandoned for a long time. Same as your house. No one wants some house where a pedo hurt little kids."

I step back as her name brings a realization forward. "He never hurt me."

He scoffs. "The whip marks on your back would disagree with you there. They may have faded, but they haven't ever gone away completely."

"There are no scars on my back, and he never touched me like that. It was Leona. It never was me."

He sighs. "This is getting old, Sam. How do you not know your own back is scarred to shit? And your dad was a fucking weirdo pervert. Trust me, the story you told the police was thorough. You had many details." He grabs me, lifting my shirt and running his hands down my back. "See, scars everywhere."

I turn my head, shaking it. "I can't see. I need a mirror." My back burns as if the injuries I didn't know about are fresh.

He points at the house. "Come on, we can get this over with and you can use the mirror in the bathroom. How the hell do you make someone not see the scars they once had? Dash is a master of something, that's for sure—mostly bullshit, I think, though." The whole conversation is coming out of our mouths too easily. We clearly have some ability to detach.

We walk in the long dried grass, next to each other. He still seems tense or angry at me for not remembering, and the closer to the house we get, the worse it is.

When my hand brushes against his, I pull it back. "I swear to you, my father hurt the other kids. I remember it, sort of."

"It doesn't matter. I hate coming here, and I hate talking about this. I had a chance to kill that filthy bastard, and I never took my chance. Still pisses me off. Coming here makes me want to burn this dump to the fucking ground so I don't have to see that look on your face ever again."

"What look?"

He takes my hand in his and squeezes. "The one where I think for half a second you think maybe you deserved to be tortured."

His words burn inside me as we round the corner of the house to find the front door is still hanging funny since Derek kicked it in. We push our way in, stopping at the entryway. It smells the same and looks the same, but the pictures are gone from the floor. My heart hurts and my lungs don't feel like they fill with enough air, like I am starved of essential things the moment we enter.

He walks to the kitchen, looking around, but as if I am attached to a string that a puppet master controls, I walk to the back of the house. Upon entering my bedroom again, I drop to my knees as though I am in a trance. I crawl along the floor to the wall at the very far end of the room and slide my hands along the edge of the wall, next to the baseboards. I catch the jagged piece of wooden floorboard I am looking for, sliding and lifting it, revealing a storage place in the floor.

I lean forward, a little scared of what's in there, only to find simple things a child would have hidden. Inside the dusty, cobweb-ridden space is a small brown box coated in enough dust that I actually believe I am the first person to open this. Beneath the layer of dust and cobwebs, I see there's a four-leaf clover pressed into the lid. I reach down, noting the way my hands shake. It feels so heavy in my hands, regardless of weighing almost nothing.

I lift it into my lap, sitting back on my butt and crossing my legs. "What is it?"

"A box I made with my mom before she died. We pressed the four-leaf clover and pasted it onto the lid with a gluey hodgepodge. I cried for the clover. I said it was now trapped for life under the glue. It would never again feel the wind on its leaves or the sun on its stem."

"Dramatic for a small kid. Ya have always seen the glass half empty, though. What did your mum say to that?" He drops onto the floor next to me with a thud. I jump from the sound, but my eyes won't leave the box.

"She said I should be happy for the clover because now it won't ever age and it won't ever rot. We preserved it in the perfect condition, so it will be lucky and beautiful forever. Always bringing me luck." Tears fill my eyes as I hear her voice with my own.

"What's inside?"

I shake my head. "I don't know." How I can recall some things and not others is driving me insane. Bravery fills me, forcing me to lift the lid. What's inside is odd.

"A necklace Mom gave me when I was three. I took it off when she died and kept it in the box like it was a treasure." I lift the small silver chain and place it on the floor. "A rubber ball Leona gave me that my father gave her. She said I could have it. He'd given her a pretty ring, and she liked that better. He had never given me anything. I wasn't even allowed to see inside the bin of the pretty clothes." It dawns on me then that my father never touched me except obviously in violence. I recall the meanness. But the bin of pretty clothes wasn't for me. Leona wore them. So did Michelle, another girl who also babysat me. She was fourteen, like Leona, when I was nine. I gulp away the horror inside me as I grab the next item. "A fortune from a fortune cookie that says *You will find a way inside of—*. I got it when my friend Nicole's family took me out for Chinese food. I'd never had it before. They said I should get a new one because it was unfinished, but I liked it the way it was. It left possibility."

Maybe it's the discomfort of being where we are or the silence of the still and haunted house. But he scoffs like we are joking about on the grass, not looking through an old box of trinkets from when I lived with my monster of a father.

When I lift the next item out, another tear drips down my cheek, leaving a streak. "A picture of me and my mom."

He takes it, inspecting it. "Ya look like her."

The very bottom of the box has a note. I lift it out, seeing instantly it's my handwriting. *Come and find me, peeping Sam!*

"What's that?"

I hand it to him, letting him try to decipher it. "I wrote that."

He nods. "I can see that. Why would ya, though?"

I shake my head. "I don't know." I lean forward, glancing into the hole again, certain there must be more.

"Well, that's fucking mysterious. Why is everything with ya a fucking puzzle? Why didn't ya just write everything down before he fucking erased your damned mind?"

"I think I must have known someone was watching me." A scowl builds on my face. "And stop cussing so much. It makes me uncomfortable, how much you swear."

His jaw drops. He shakes his head. "Well, now I've heard it all."

Ignoring him and drumming my fingers along the wooden floor, I think about the sentence. "It could be an anagram. I mean, it's sort of random to call me peeping Sam." But saying the phrase brings with it a memory, exactly the way "plain Jane" did.

I close my eyes and suddenly it's all there, filling my brain.

I'm small, very small, maybe eight at most. I chase a bunny under the house. Our house is on blocks like a trailer. Father's been digging a basement. I creep under there, my fingers digging into the dank grass and weeds.

A noise fills the air. The sound of a whimper. I follow it to the front of the house where the steps are. There's a hole in the floor, a notch out of the wood so small I haven't seen it from the inside of the house. But here in the dark I can see light from inside the house shining down into the mucky dead grass. I lift my face, up into the floorboards, no longer interested in the bunny, and put my eye to the notch hole. Leona, my babysitter, is in there. I can't see her face, but I know the sound of her voice. She's making a funny sound, but whatever she's doing, I can't see it. Father's back is to me. He's got something in his hands. He mutters encouragements, repeating the word *diddling* like it means something. He sounds different with her, like he likes her.

I gag, trying desperately to snap out of the memory, but this one has me and it's not letting go.

I watch my father's back, completely confused about what is happening. They make sounds and do things I don't see. Clothes ruffle and bodies shuffle, and the dark and light mix in the shadows and angles I can't catch with my prying eyes. She gets up and walks to my bedroom. It's then I catch a glimpse of the pretty clothes she has on. They're from the bin I'm not allowed to touch.

Hurrying back to the backyard, I catch a glimpse of her changing in my bedroom from where I'm running through the field. He likes her better than me. It's then I realize it.

From then on, when she or Michelle came over to babysit and I was sent outside to play, I would hurry under the house. There in the dark I would wait at the notch to watch the things they did for the camera. It was like a train wreck; I couldn't look away. It made me feel funny. I knew it was wrong, all of it.

The memory fades into the fog and mud in my head as I blink tears from my eyes. "I lied about my father."

He wraps himself around me, hugging me tightly to him. "No you didn't. He was a monster."

I nod. "He was, but he never molested me. He molested the girls who babysat me." I am ashamed of myself. My body curls into his, desperate to hide from the truth, but I know that's where the secrets are hidden. They're buried in the places I am most ashamed to talk about or share. When I told myself to go back, this is the place I meant. I take his hand, pulling him to the living room where the notch in the floor still sits in the corner. "He did it all here, in this living room. He paid them to babysit, but he always stayed home. He paid them heaps of money to star in the shows." My cheeks are bright red and my eyes are burning. "I watched through this hole from under the house. I never told anyone for a year. He did it all the time. The pictures and movies didn't show faces clearly. No one could tell who the kid in the picture was, just that it was a kid." I turn, looking at the fireplace. My feet move, even though my brain is screaming for them to stop. I reach for the brick I know will move, revealing the hiding place. When I pull it back, the papers from the floor are stuffed in there. The papers Derek showed me before. They have always been here. They never were in the folder or found by the police. One picture grabs at me from the stack. It's a girl's mouth with a cherry in it. A bitter smile owns my face as I recall Michelle teaching me to do it when she babysat me. I want to judge myself for the fact I'm ever so slightly excited that I didn't learn the trick in a brothel somewhere.

Rory gets up and walks to the fireplace. He reaches into the hole, pulling out the papers. He gags slightly, turning his face away from the sickening images. From the look on his face I have to assume this might be more than he can handle, but then he shakes his head. "This isn't your fault."

I hate that he is seeing this side of me. "It is. I never told anyone what he was doing until he caught me doing it, touching myself in the living room. I was just about ten. He beat me, so I told the teacher everything he had done to Michelle and Leona, but I made it sound like he did it to me. I told them every tiny detail, but it wasn't ever done to me."

I hate myself.

I hate this house.

I hate Derek because I know he knows this and has used it all to play with my head.

Rory sits with the knowledge inside himself. I can see him processing and contemplating it all. "I have to burn this house to the ground. We have to leave now."

I shake my head. "There's one place I need to go first." I turn and walk out the front door to the hatch at the side of the house. The basement was built when my father got out of prison. I lift up the doors, letting them fall away to the sides. Rory is next to me when I take the stairs into the darkness. He pulls out his cell phone, making it a flashlight. The cellar is so creepy, but there is one place I have to see. I turn to the right, walking to the front where I used to be able to see under the stairs. I look up, seeing the notch hole in the floor like it always was. But there in the dusty darkness I see something that was never there before—a VHS taped to the underside of the wood.

It's the only secret I have ever kept with myself. The only secret I have kept from Derek.

I pry the tape loose, dragging it from the wood. Dust and particles drop from it, but I finally get it free, handing it to Rory as I close my eyes and try to step away from the dust.

Something hits me in the back of the head, making everything black.

13. THE VIEW FROM BELOW

Smoke wakes me. My head is throbbing, and as far as I can see in the dark, the air is filled with dust. I squint, trying to see where I am. It takes several seconds of replaying the last few images I have in my head before I realize where I am.

I am on the dirty floor of the cellar, and the house above is on fire. Looking up I see light in the notch hole. Something moves up there in the smoke, making the light vanish and then come again. My head is pounding and my heart is racing but I get up, dragging myself to the notch. I sway from the trauma done to my head, grabbing quickly onto a joist to stabilize myself. I lean forward, peeking through the notch hole like I did all the time as a child, and once again I see something I don't expect—a gray eye looking back at me.

I jump, still staring at it. It moves like he has narrowed his gaze. "I missed you all day, baby."

I shake my head as tears start to trickle down my cheeks. "Why are you doing this to me? Where's Rory?"

He laughs. "You still believe he's on your side? He hits you in the head and he's still the good guy? Jesus, Jane. What do I have to do to prove I love you?"

My eyes narrow, matching the look on his face, I'm sure. "Give me back my video."

He chuckles. "Jane, I never wanted the video. You were always the prize for me. That was their big obsession. Now come out from under there before the house falls on you." His gray eye is gone, and the light is back.

I turn, still squinting to see better. Suddenly, a light flashes at the entrance to the cellar. It moves like it's in a hand, swaying it back and forth at a concert.

I have two options—die in this fire or go to the man I believe is responsible for it all. It's a no-brainer, but it's also like selling my soul to the devil. I stumble through the smoke to the entrance, taking his hand and letting him pull me to safety. He lifts me into his arms and runs away. All my hate and anger are burning up with the house behind us. Everything becomes less painful, seeing the billowing smoke coming from the haunted house that Derek has left burning in our wake. I blink, but the view still continues to shrink away as if my body ignores my fears, and again I lose consciousness.

When I wake there is a sound, a song or humming. I recognize the tune.

"Once in a while, send me a smile. Make me see who you want me to be. If you'd only listen to the sounds of my heart beating for you." Derek's voice singing the tune to the taunting song picks at me. I've heard it before, in his voice. "Listen, listen to the wind and stone. Listen, listen to the sounds of old. Listen, listen as my hopes are drowned. Listen, listen to the sounds that bullets make of blood and bones. Where will you run today? How will you ever get away? Our love is meant to stay."

I shudder as a memory floods my mind, taking all of me into it.

The song wakes me. I stumble from the bed into the dark hall-way in search of its source. His voice is new to me for only a second as memories flit about my head and recognition occurs halfway through the darkness. He is the man I love and trust—my father.

The song is odd. I don't recognize it. He repeats it using the same taunting melody. When I get around the corner there's a door with a sliver of silver light shining from it. The song is coming from the crack, echoing inside the light within the room that becomes bluer as I get closer. The color makes my bare feet on the marble floor feel as if it's colder than it actually is. I shudder as the creepy chorus plays again off the pale-blue walls.

"Listen, listen to the wind and stone. Listen, listen to the sounds of old. Listen, listen as my hopes are drowned. Listen, listen to the sounds that bullets make of blood and bones. Where will you run today? How will you ever get away? Our love is meant to stay."

When I peek through the slit, the cool blue paint on the walls and ivory floors contract remarkably with the spatters of red all over. My father, a man who has never shown me a moment of love or kindness, is cutting up something bloody. A hand lies on the floor, pointing at the wall on the other side of the room. There is no arm attached. It takes several seconds for the images to compute, but he hums and sings the chorus again.

"Listen, listen to the wind and stone. Listen, listen to the sounds of old. Listen, listen as my hopes are drowned. Listen, listen to the sounds that bullets make of blood and bones. Where will you run today? How will you ever get away? Our love is meant to stay."

I gasp, backing away. When I turn I trip, making the music stop. The warm singing in the cold room ceases, and hollow footsteps take its place.

"Jane?"

I scramble to my feet, spinning around.

My eyes pop open, as I come back from my memories. The song

was his. The weirdness was never mine. The shit wrong with me—the cherry and the creepy song and the memory loss—are not mine. They are my father's, and God help me, but I have fallen in love with a man just like him.

It takes a second to come out of the weird dream. The room I'm in reminds me of a place I've been. It has a soft bed with a fluffy pillow and pretty paint color, but I know it's fake, like our sanity.

The door opens, with his smiling face poking through the opening. "You're awake? I figured you would need a bit more sleep. You haven't been sleeping or eating enough. You need that. You need to stay calm."

"I need answers, all of them. I need to know now, right now, what this is. Why did you burn the house and attack Rory? Did you leave him at the house?"

He pushes the door open as if he's freeing me, making me more comfortable, which I think is his intention. "You volunteered for this."

"What? Where's Rory?" He offers me his hand. I don't hesitate—I climb from the bed and storm past him. "Stop coddling me, Derek. I'm not your fucking toy."

He chuckles and follows me down the hall. We're in a hotel. It's a suite with a large living room. I sit down on the couch, holding my hands wide. "What the hell is going on?"

He strolls calmly to the TV, hooking up a VCR.

"Is that Pat's?"

He nods, dropping to his knees and turning the TV and VCR on. The wide flat-screen TV, which couldn't be more opposite from the VCR connected to it, turns on. My face, my face from before, appears on the screen, frozen. Derek comes and sits next to me, patting my leg.

I shove his hand off me, looking at him with a glare. "What is this?"

"Your VHS. I stole it first a while ago. When you were sleep-walking once you told me where it was. I let that asshole Rory take the fake one I made from this one, missing all the good stuff, of course. Do you know how hard it was to make it dusty like that?"

I pause, completely stunned. "You are insane."

He shrugs. "I know." He presses "play" with the remote he stole from Pat's house with her ancient VCR, left over from when I was a teenager. The picture runs clearer as he hits the button.

"You found us." My smile is wide and coated in red lipstick. I brush my blonde hair behind my ears and nod. "I knew you would know the only place in the world I would ever hide something." The light in my eyes dims. "It's the only place no one would know about, unless I trusted them more than anything in the world." I glance next to me, like I hear something but the camera can't see it.

I look back at the camera, lowering my voice. "I've found something out. Something that's big. All this time I've been hunting down Benjamin Dash has proved to be enlightening. He's part of a CIA operation that takes requests or cleanup jobs as favors to other organizations. He's part of the cleaning team for cleaning teams— part of something the world has no clue about. And the worst part is we knew all along. Our own government runs this. Dash was selected because of his theories. He's built a team of people who can become like psychopaths, and enjoy the end of someone's life. They all like to watch the spark go out." Her eyes narrow, like she's fighting emotions. "Anyway, he's a doctor, and the intel I recovered on him and the program didn't do what it was supposed to. Essentially, I showed up the government and its evil plotting and mind screwing with completely innocent people. The evidence against the government is in a safe-deposit box in a bank in Turin, Italy, in the Cassa Depositi e Prestiti. The key is in the place where you hid from the monsters. It's the safest place I could think to put it." She looks down for a brief second, shaking her head. "Sam, or whatever your name is now, let the past go. No good is going to come from opening that box. It already ruined our lives. It already ruined everything. Just let it go, trust me." She looks up at the camera, nodding. "Let Father go. He was a weak man who preyed on the innocent, and nothing we did when we were little can be blamed on us. We were a product of our environment. That's what I've learned in all of this. Learn to love and let go and be a strong person for the right reasons. It's something we never have been very good at."

The video ends, ejecting the VHS when it's done. I look at Derek. "Explain all of that in really dumb terms."

A knock at the door startles me, but he stands casually and walks to it. A man in a white jacket wheels in a cart of food, leaving us with it. Instantly, I can smell chicken Parm. Derek lifts the lids, making steam flood the top of the table. The food is incredibly hot and fresh, making my mouth water immediately. He carries over a silver tray, placing it on the coffee table in front of me. I take the silverware, nodding. "This is evil. You know how I feel about food."

He chuckles. "I thought it was only *my* food."

I take the first bite of the noodles after dragging it through the marinara and crispy cheese. My eyes close on their own, and a moan escapes my lips.

"That hurts my feelings."

I nod. "It should. This is fantastic."

"Better than mine?" He sits across from me on the floor with his silver tray of steak and potatoes. A meal more fitting for him.

"Explain."

He cuts into the juicy rare steak. I have to look away or I'll lose my appetite. "There is so little to explain. You know it all. We fell in love; I never lied about that." He takes his bite, lifting his gray-green stare to mine. Watching him chew the meat, with the image of him butchering the man in the stark blue room, takes my appetite away. He nods. "You fell in love with a monster. I never hid what I was or what I did. You knew it all—the only person in the world who had seen the place inside me where there should have been a soul." He swallows, making me gag. He points his steak knife at me. "This is why you made me take your memories. You couldn't eat meat. You couldn't see me eat anything. You couldn't sleep without a light most nights, even if I was there. You couldn't, and that was the answer to everything. We'd be in a café in France and I'd ask a question and you'd lose the color in your face, staring at a man who looked similar to your dad. You wouldn't even hear me. You were lost in the shame you felt for it all. I tried to explain to you that sometimes we are born in a trap that's already set and we are going to lose no matter how hard we fight it."

Tears run down my cheeks.

"At least you can cry now. That's a new development."

I sniffle, wiping my eyes. The plate of food in front of me is delicious—I know it is. The man in front of me is devoted—I know he is. The world is so large we could get lost in it if we wanted to—I know that. But the trap has still got me. I am still losing against it. Only this time I'm not going to keep losing. I refuse. I push the plate away, determined this will be the last time I lose anything. "I want to end this, all of it."

"Then you have to go to Italy and open the box."

I cock an eyebrow. "You saw the video. I told myself not to do that."

"That's the only way for this to end—take away the thing they want."

I shake my head. "There has to be another way."

The look in his eyes turns grave. "You and me dead is the other solution they have."

"The stuff in that box is protecting us from death."

He sighs. "No it isn't. We aren't safe as long as we have it. It needs to go away, and then *we* need to go away."

It just doesn't seem like the right choice. I shake my head again. "What if the people who want the information against you are all dead? Will you be free then? Who is it?"

He looks a bit defeated when he sighs and says their names: "Randall, Rory, and my contact, Don Nobleman. The files in the system on us are all blank. They don't keep work orders on the things we do, and every death looks to be an accident, so there is no proof." His eyes narrow with amusement as if he's laughing at a joke on the inside. "Apart from the evidence you gathered. You were the only one who was ever able to do it."

"So if they are gone and we destroy the evidence in the safety-deposit box, technically you and I are free?"

"Technically."

One thing picks at me. "Why did I keep the evidence?"

The grin he's been playing with finally spreads across his face. "Because you were going to do the right thing and bring me in. You needed to gather as much evidence of my sins as you could manage before bringing me in. It would make my insurance I keep on the government null and void. No one believes a guilty serial killer about anything. With proof I was a savage, they could lock me up, and anything I tried to use against them would look like the mad ravings of a lunatic."

My stomach drops. "Did I start a relationship with you for the job?"

He nods slowly, and the humor leaves his face. "That, and you found out something in those files that made you realize you couldn't kill me." There's a small part of me that fears he took me as his trophy when he found out who I was. It's a logical fear in a situation like this one. I don't think I will ever know if he forced me into sacrificing my memories and past so he could keep me his prisoner. I have to assume he's on my side.

"What happened at my father's house? Why did you light the fire?"

He shakes his head. "I never. I drove like a madman to the house, arriving as he had set the fire. Randall was there. They had the VHS. Rory wanted to bring you in, but Randall said you had betrayed them and were nothing more than a loose end. They had released you to find the VHS. It was all they needed. They left you there to die."

"How did you know about the notch hole?"

He swallows hard. "There was a notch hole at my house too." He has never spoken of his life before. "We discussed our worst sins once." He leaves it there. I can see he's not going to talk about it more. "I think you should go to Italy and get this over with."

"No."

He shrugs. "Then what's the plan?"

"No, we kill Rory, Randall, and that Don guy. Then we go back to the West Coast and we start over. I'm never going to Italy, and I'm never opening that box. It's my insurance."

His eyes widen. "You want to start over again? It's the third time."

"I know, but maybe it'll be the lucky time." There are a thousand things hovering in my mind that I need to know or argue over, but this isn't the time for it.

"What about the evidence? Leaving it there is a mistake." He gives me a look.

"We leave it there until I think we are safe to go and see what it is." Part of me is scared to even look.

He nods. "Sounds like a plan." He looks down at his dinner and groans. "What a waste."

"You won't finish it?"

His eyes dart to my meal. "Not if you won't finish yours." It makes me smile. He's distant and cold and a killer in several different ways, but he's still sweet.

I really must have lost my mind.

14. SEE JANE KILL

The dark shadow we hide in makes me nervous. He places a hand on the small of my back, leaning in to whisper in my ear, "Jane, the dark is your friend. Only in the dark can you hide and sneak and watch. The dark is on our side."

It's chilling, but I know he's right. We creep along the side of the large house. It was a fourteen-hour drive here, but it will be one tick off the list of people who can make us disappear. I have come to an us-against-them mindset.

He reaches around me, opening the door with a turn of the knob. He lifts a gloved finger to his lips. I nod.

We creep inside. I can't believe a man from the CIA would sleep with his house unlocked. The sensors detecting movement in the kitchen and hallways might be the reason. I freeze when I see one, but Derek steps up to a panel and punches in a four-digit number. The light on the panel turns to green. He gives me a grin.

We sneak along the dark hallway, tiptoeing up the stairs where he tiptoes directly to a specific room, again turning the knob silently.

He creeps into the room, where a man snores and a woman breathes deeply.

He drops to his knees at the bedside of the sleeping man, pulling back the covers slightly. He slips a needle from his jacket, shaking a tiny vial. He fills the syringe with the liquid from the vial. Then he takes a piece of wood and a small packet from his pocket. He wipes the arm with the cloth from the packet, numbing the skin. He drags the piece of sharp wood along the spot he's numbed and injects the needle into him, covering the needle hole with a second drag of the wood. He pulls a plastic bag from his pocket, placing all the items into the plastic bag so silently I'm actually baffled. Baffled and disgusted. The fact that a man is about to be killed makes me feel varying emotions, at least one of which is sadness. He's lying in his bed, asleep and snoring next to his wife. He's at peace. He has kids and a dog. He's a man, a regular man, and we are here to end that.

I don't like it.

But it's us against them, and he's on their side. My freedom depends on his death, whether I like it or not.

Derek gets up, leaving the room, but I stand there, wishing I could tell the dying man to kiss his wife good-bye. I feel sick for them both. Derek comes back, taking my gloved hand in his and pulling me from the room. We slip down the stairs, an argument brewing in my head as we exit the house after setting the sensor alarm again.

"What was that? He's still up there snoring away. Why did you do it this way? It seems sick to leave him like that, a ticking time bomb for his wife."

"He takes a sleeping pill at night. There's no waking him until his eight hours are up. That specific poison mimics the flesh-eating disease. He was with his family in Virginia Beach yesterday. There was a news report that several beaches along the East Coast had the flesh-eating bacteria, vibrio, in the waters. Now, to the common coroner or doctor, he has flesh-eating disease. I would diagnose that.

The poison will kill him in the next two hours and eat away at the spot on his arm. He'll die looking like he has suffered a major onset during the evening." He smiles wide, making my heart skip beats.

I don't know what to say. He's a sick, sick man. And yet, he's a genius. We turn and leave the property as I fight the desperate need to vomit. "How did you know his alarm code?"

He glances back at me as we enter the woods. "There are some people in this world who should never be trifled with. They should be left to live in peace because they are far too dangerous for the average human being." He opens the car door for me as we reach the back road we parked on. "I am one of those people. When I decide to kill someone I learn everything. I have several possible outcomes mapped out in my head. I force myself to use the kindest means possible, depending on the person. Don was a good man. He never screwed me over on purpose. He just knew it was time to retire me. His version of retirement and mine differ. I let him retire his way." He closes my door, and I realize he isn't boasting. He isn't like that. He is sincere in his words and his actions.

We drive to an older part of DC, where he parks next to a building that is a bit rough for my liking. He gets out so I follow. When he enters the building from an unlocked door on the side, I pause. I don't want to go into the run-down building, but the streets surrounding us aren't any better. He pokes his head back out of the door, giving me a look. "It's nicer inside."

I follow him into the building, trying not to flip out at the slight noises in the distant corners I cannot see. It's a warehouse type of building, not an apartment. It isn't at all what I imagined. We climb some metal stairs to a large door. When he opens it the sight confuses me. It's a beautiful flat that should be where the office for the warehouse is. He holds the door open, looking smug. "See!"

"Look, you've been lying to me for a long time. You murdered Ronald; you were putting my aunt on a flight to Colorado, not Austria, where we were going; you murdered people for fun and for a living; and you've erased my mind twice, but there are things in there I can't explain. I remember torturing my father. You've told me I kill cats in my sleep, but I don't think that's true. So wipe that smug look off your face." I stalk into the flat, slumping down into a chair. I'm exhausted and starving.

He presses his back against the closed door. "I never killed Ronald. You did. I wasn't lying." He looks down. "You get confused sometimes. It's only since the amnesia set in. You sleepwalk, but it isn't sleepwalking. It's real. You're awake, and you are old Sam and paranoid. Very paranoid."

My eyes lower to my hands. "What did I do to him?"

"You stabbed him. I followed you, but I got there too late. So I stabbed over and over, making the wounds inconsistent. I took you home and I cleaned you and put you back to bed."

"The next night I woke covered in blood again."

He nods. "I don't know what you killed. I was truly at work. I thought since the threat was gone, old Sam would be at peace again. She only comes out when there's a threat. I keep your world as peaceful as I can. You can't run into people you might know, and you can't get stressed in any way. It makes it worse."

"But I haven't done it since I started finding everything out. I haven't been sleepwalking."

He shakes his head. "No. It doesn't mean you won't."

I never imagined I would be as much a threat as he is, or even more of one. "Are you scared I'll hurt you?"

"Sometimes I worry about it, but I like to give you the benefit of the doubt, considering who we both are in this." His tone is dark and eerie. It matches us. We are both dark and eerie.

"Am I still a murderer if I don't remember doing it?"

He shakes his head.

"When did I torture my father?"

He winces. "You didn't."

"I remember—"

"The man looked like your dad. He was a man from Paris who made the mistake of touching you in a way you didn't want. He looked similar to your dad. You didn't kill him, I did."

"Oh God. I'm an animal." None of it feels real. None of it makes sense. "Did I really kill cats?" He nods slowly as my entire world falls apart. "I'm an animal."

He walks to me, dropping to his knees on the hardwood floor in front of me. "You are a sweet person. A good person. If you were awake and fully conscious, you wouldn't hurt an innocent person. Trust me."

"Why did it start when you erased my memory?"

He shakes his head. "I don't know. I exhausted the research on it, but there is no way to specifically answer questions about the brain and the subconscious. We are more than we know. Layers are in there, in our minds. We can't always see inside the layers. We can't stop being who we are in there."

"Like you with the killing?" Did I just justify his being a killer? Does it matter, with the track record I have?

He lifts me up, scooping me into his arms. He kisses the side of my face, breathing me in. "I love you, Jane. I loved you when you were Andrea, I loved you as Sam. I will love you with whatever name you choose for the next time. I wasn't lying to you when I said we found each other in the dark and we made light. That's what you are for me. You are possibility and light and love and everything I never had before I met you."

Andrea? I wrap my arms around him. "I don't know how to be a normal girl. I just want to be normal."

He shakes his head. "What's normal? We were raised by the normal people out there in the world. Every house has secrets, even if it looks normal on the outside. Every house has a notch hole, Jane.

Look what normal made us." His eyes are more green than gray, shining with what might be the light we make together.

I press my face into his, letting my forehead rest on his cheek. "Can we just be the people we are in here?"

He nods, carrying me to a bedroom with no lights on. It's dark, and in the shadows I see things. There are hands reaching for me, monsters slithering about in the blackest places, and sharp teeth awaiting me under the bed. But I am the scariest monster in the room, so I'm not afraid of them. It dawns on me then that the reason I don't need a night-light with him isn't because I feel safer, it's because I see the reality of the situation. He is my dose of perspective. He makes me see that I don't need to fear the other things in the room. They need to fear me.

He pulls my shirt off, tossing it into the oblivion made of shadows. His warm hands trail along my skin as he dips his face, sliding his tongue into my mouth. I suck it, caressing and waiting for the storm I know is coming. Every movement and caress is too soft. He slips a hand down my body to my hip. His finger traces along the front of me slowly, pressing into my abdomen as if it were a massage. He touches nothing but the safe places, making my nipples and pussy desperate for affection. I run my hands up his taut body, dragging his shirt off too. He dips a hand between my thighs, brushing either side of my legs but still avoiding the one place I want touched so badly. Not waiting for him to come around to my way of seeing things, I undo his pants, sliding my hand down into his boxers, gripping his rock-hard shaft. He sucks his breath, still tormenting me with his fingers and lips.

I change my grip, stroking him softly, twisting with my hand at the top. He growls into our kiss, biting down on my lip. It makes me grin to be in control of his pleasure.

He doesn't struggle for the control back, he just takes it, slipping a finger straight into me. I'm soaked from the anticipation of it all, so his movements are well lubed. He exits, sliding a second finger into me. I moan, feeling him stretch me. My grip on his cock tightens, jerking more than caressing.

He moans into my mouth, but I can't continue the kiss. My head falls back as we kneel on the bed, chest to chest, stroking each other.

He takes advantage of the position and pushes me back onto the bed as he slides down my body, kissing his way to my mound. He slides between my thighs, spreading them wide and placing soft kisses on the inside of my legs. I tremble with excitement as he lowers his head farther, licking my entire slit. His tongue drags along the lips teasingly, before plunging inside me. I cry out, writhing my hips so I take more of the penetration than he perhaps intends. He fucks with his tongue, in and out, while rubbing my clit with his thumb. A finger joins his tongue inside me, moving with the rubbing of my clit. Sounds leave my lips, but he shifts positions suddenly, sliding his body over mine and sticking the head of his waiting cock in my parted lips. I open my mouth, letting him slide it as far as I can take it. He tries to push it farther at the exact moment he speeds all his movements up. I cry out in a gargled moan as my body twitches against him with the greatest release I've ever had. His hips continue to thrust into my mouth, nearly assaulting my face as the flood continues to wash over me, and his hands slow. He starts spanking my clit, driving the finishing orgasm home with vibration.

He strokes us both, his thrusting cock and my vibrating pussy, softly as I finish clenching against his fingers. He pulls himself from my mouth. A string of spit trails along me as he moves between my thighs again, only this time he sticks my feet on his shoulders, lifting my ass in the air. The soft and sweet lovemaking is a thing of the past. We are fucking, and I am near praying it never ends. He runs his cock's head up and down my slit before entering me roughly. With my ass in the air he buries his cock, making me take every inch and filling me too full. His body stretches mine, but his thrusts maintain the strength they started with. He grips my hips, holding me in the air and dragging me up and down his cock with his mighty pounding. The pressure builds again as the vibration of the slapping balls and thrusting cock fill me. I feel myself clenching as the power of a second orgasm builds. I am close, meeting his thrusts and pushing with my own body, but he pulls out of me before I can finish. He sits up, flipping me onto my stomach. Again he grips my hips, but this time he drags my ass back to where he sits, arching me so he can shove himself back inside me. His fingers bite into my hips, almost hurting, but the pain has joined the pleasure and every sensation makes me higher. I scream into the sheets and blankets as the orgasm returns almost instantly, not requiring a buildup. When I come he pounds against me savagely. His fingers dig in harder as he groans, still moving with a pace I cannot keep up with. I am lost in the rhythm, drooling on the bed and bleating like a sheep when I feel him pulsate inside me. He jerks into me several times before collapsing on top of me. He kisses along my sweat-laden back. "I love you." His words are breathy and weak.

I nod into my own sweat and drool, agreeing but unable to find the words.

When we wake in the morning, light has flooded the bedroom. It's disturbingly bright. How we've slept as long as we have is some kind of miracle or testament to how tired we both were.

He snuggles into me, kissing along my neck. "Where to now?"

"Breakfast, and then we find Randall."

He nods. "I know where he is."

Nothing he says surprises me now. We dress in silence, not talking about the exquisite sex we had. It was so different from the years of lovemaking at a slow and casual pace. I don't know how to bring it up. I don't want to plan our sex life, but I don't want to go back. We walk to the car, hand in hand. I don't know how it happened, maybe it was during the mind-blowing orgasms, but I don't care about the flaws in the system. I don't care who we are. I offer him a sly smile. "What are you thinking about?"

He purses his lips. "I want to say the sex last night because, seriously, it's been on my mind a lot, but I have to be honest. I'm thinking that it doesn't matter that we are the couple most likely to blow up the world just by being together. I don't care that we are two peas in a pod who should probably be medicated, and I don't care that you are a liability and I cannot ever satisfy the cravings inside me. I just want this, but I don't know how to make it happen. I don't know how we can be together, as broken as we are, and not fuck it up."

He doesn't swear often, but when he does it's usually because he's being very serious.

"I have a terrible feeling we will just keep spinning on this wheel and we won't ever be free of the truth that keeps us prisoners of the traps we were raised in."

I lift his hand to my lips, placing a soft kiss and lingering for a moment. "Then we die on the wheel."

He grins back. "That's a ridiculous answer."

"Well, like you said, we are the couple most likely to destroy the world by being together. I say we take our chances, and if we go down, we take everyone with us."

His brow knits together in a worried stare. "You really are a twisted individual."

I nod. There's really nothing else to add to it. The darkness of my prior life has caught up with me. I don't think there is any going back.

He drives us to a business as we discuss the plan several times over. I don't think it'll work, but he's certain it will. I don't recognize it, but I have a feeling I have been here before. He gets a bag from the trunk when he parks in the alley. He hands me a dark wig with the hair in a bun. He places a pair of glasses on the console for me. I almost grin over the glasses, but then he sets out a sticker-looking thing with a brown dot on a piece of white paper. I frown. "What's this?"

He grins. "Your disguise." He puts the brown dot on my face, making a mole where Cindy Crawford has hers.

I wrinkle my nose. "I hate moles."

He nods. "I know." He pulls on a gray wig and a pair of glasses. They're not cute dark frames like mine. His are wire frames like an old man's. I drag my own hair into a bun and pull on the dark wig. He hands me bright-red lipstick. I flip the visor down and open the mirror so I can see when I smear the lipstick on. The reflection makes me pause, realizing how chic I look. "I should dye my hair this color."

"You look good as a medium brown. This is very dark, almost black. It really makes you pale."

I scowl. "Wow, tell me what you really think."

He nods. "I did." Clearly he doesn't get the joke. He pulls a sweater out and hands it to me. I slip it over my pale tank top and button it up. It's cold here, so the sweater won't be too hot. He hands me a pair of heels. I pull my feet from my sneakers and rip my socks off. He shrugs on a hideous old-man sweater to go with his black pants. I didn't even notice he was wearing them. He nods. "Now, when we get inside I want you to go to the front desk and ask the lady the questions. Try to stay Spanish for as long as you can. The secretary at the front desk of the electric company is an idiot. She doesn't speak Spanish, but she lied on her résumé. The only way to work for the government in DC is to speak a second language, at minimum."

I sigh, already embarrassed at the idiot I'm going to make of myself. He hands me my visitor pass and gets out of the car. He grabs a cane from the back and starts his very slow progression down the alley. I get out, clicking my high heels along the concrete. I pass him, ignoring his existence completely.

When I get to the large building, I walk through the front doors, feeling the memories attempting to come back in. I block it out. I don't need to stand like a moron in the middle of the floor as my head fills with all sorts of memories that don't matter right now.

I scan my card and walk to the escalator. The ride up is so familiar I feel nauseated. At the top of the shiny white area, I turn right. The girl at the front desk with the huge doors behind her smiles at me when she sees me. She's friendlier than a front-desk girl should be. In Spanish I ask her if the weather has been good in DC, as I have only just arrived.

She immediately stops smiling, bites her lip, and nods.

I ask her if she is a flying monkey.

She nods again.

I roll my eyes, hiding the fact I'm starting to feel bitchy for doing this to her. She smiles weakly. I point at the door behind me and ask her if there is a Mabel who works there. She is my grandmother, and I need her recipe for lemon loaf.

She shakes her head.

Finally, acting as if I am completely annoyed, I ask her if she speaks Spanish. I'm stunned I can.

She nods. I slap a hand down on the counter and call her a lying pig.

"Ma'am, please don't get upset. We will work with you to correct this. Clearly you've been told to come to the wrong place." Her accent is similar to Pat's.

I slap my hand down again, asking God why he has cursed us with stupid Americans.

She stands up. "Did you just call me a stupid Americano?"

I lunge forward, acting like I might come at her, using the thickest Spanish accent I can. "You stupid Americano!"

She grabs my hands, slapping them down on the desk. "You will not talk to me like that. I don't know who you think you are, but you're lucky us Americanos let you Mexicans into the US. Damned foreigners. You have to come to America and speak American, not Mexican."

I feign shock. "I no Mexican!" I'm not sure I'm doing the Spaniards of the world any favors talking like an idiot.

A security guard comes through the door. "Is there a problem here?"

The girl's face is flushed. "No, no, sir. We're just having us a little disagreement. She's at the wrong counter, and I tried telling her that."

He gives me a look. "This is a secure area. We don't allow visitors in here."

In Spanish I tell him she's a savage who called me a Mexican and said I speak Mexican. I add that she called me a foreigner and refused to greet me in Spanish, even though the sign right there says Spanish is an acceptable language at this counter. I say that she doesn't speak a word of Spanish and his company is racist.

His cheeks become the color of hers. He understands every word I speak. He turns, pointing at the doors behind him. "Mallory, go inside and tell Mr. Kip that you might not have told the whole truth on your application."

She swallows hard. "What is she accusing me of? I did nothing!"

I lean across the desk. "If you speak Spanish you know what I accuse you of."

Her eyes narrow. She turns quickly, storming through the large doors behind us. The security guard has friends suddenly. Several of them are there, surrounding me. The man sighs. "I am terribly sorry, ma'am. We are not racist, I assure you. Now is there something I can help you with?"

I shake my head, hoping it has been enough of a diversion since every security guard on the floor has been alerted to me and my situation. "I have wrong counter. I know this now. I am looking for Aunt Mabel."

He scowls. "There's a Mabel in here."

My heart drops. "Mabel Manuel?"

He shakes his head. "No, you do have the wrong area." He holds a hand out. "There are a dozen floors in the building. Maybe call your aunt to see if you have the right floor."

I offer a small wave. "Thank you, kind sir." I turn and walk past the crowd of them that have gathered in the hall.

My heart is racing, my stomach is burning, and I have never felt more alive. I turn and walk back to the escalator, taking out the cell phone Derek gave me earlier. I dial a random number as I take the escalator down. I pause on the main floor, noticing how many of them are still watching me. An answering machine kicks on, but I talk like I have reached my aunt. I speak animatedly in Spanish, slapping myself on the forehead like I have come in the wrong building. I walk out the front doors, looking to the right and nodding as if she has given me the directions again. I walk into the next building and take the elevator to the third floor. It's an accounting firm with a large staff. I take the stairs when I get to the floor and leave through the back alley. When I get back into the fresh air I pull off the wig and ditch the mole and glasses. I pull off the sweater and wrap everything in it. I fluff my hair so it's huge. I walk to the Dumpster behind the building and place the sweater and other items in it. I walk the long way back to the car, praying he's doing okay.

I start the car with the key he gave me when he handed me the phone as he drilled me on the details of the plan. The drive to the park five blocks over is tense. It isn't that I think he's going to get caught—he's a genius. It's that Randall is a smart man. He's been the head of our operation for a long time. He might know things about Derek. Things I told him, that Derek won't be prepared for.

I sit in the car, waiting for a long time. Eventually I get out, standing in the freezing air with nothing but my tank top and jeans on. I lie on the hood, like it's a summer day and not an evening in late fall.

The clouds look like horses. I swear they always do.

When the sun sets I start to really worry. I pace, walking around the car with my teeth chattering and my skin turning a pale-blue color.

Finally, when I can't take it any longer, I get back into the car and wait for him in there. It's completely dark in the park when I admit he's in trouble. I don't want to. I want him to be okay, and I want him to come back to me. But I can't deny the fact of the matter is that he is clearly caught or worse.

I drive around the city twice, like he told me to, and head back to the apartment. When I get there I have to remind myself I am the craziest monster in the world and nothing in the dark warehouse is going to be as nuts as me. I creep into the dark, jumping several times when noises taunt me from their hiding place in the shadows.

Climbing the stairs to the flat makes me nervous, and not just because I have the entire warehouse behind me. While I have turned my back on the darkness and made myself vulnerable, I hardly notice it because the door is open to the flat and the light from it is flooding the metal stairs.

15. MAGICAL KEY OF DOOM

It's insane, but I swear I can feel the heat from the lights inside the flat. When I get to the top of the stairs I wish I had a gun. There's blood on the doorknob. I reach up, pushing the door open farther, revealing more dots of blood spattered across the foyer.

I hurry inside, expecting to find him wounded.

I don't expect him to be on the floor unconscious, but he is. I'm nearly blind with worry and fear as I dash across the room, skidding on my knees to his side. I push him over, finding a bullet hole in his side that's made a puddle far too large for a person to survive. I lay him on his back, pressing down on the injury. He stirs, wincing. "Your hands are freezing!" He speaks with a breathy whisper.

"What happened?" My voice is cracked and falling apart, just like everything else.

He shakes his head, grinning. "He switched places where he keeps his gun. I assumed either the bar or the desk, but he put one in the bathroom. He was clearly getting paranoid."

"Was? Did you kill Randall?"

He lifts a hand to my cheek. "I saw the light leave his eyes."

I push harder on the wound as hot liquid seeps onto my cold hands. "We have to get you to the hospital."

He shakes his head, swallowing like it's painful. "It's a stomach shot. I had a window of time. I could see you one last time, or I could get to the hospital and leave you to worry about me." He smiles weakly. "I couldn't stand to see you vulnerable and scared. What if you went back for me?"

Tears start to fill my eyes, again trying to make it so I can't see everything. "No. You have to see a doctor."

He laughs, cringing in pain. "I am a doctor, let me tell you. No one lives this amount of time with a stomach wound. I'm on borrowed time."

I slump over the wound, shaking my head. "Borrow a little more. Don't leave me."

He lifts a red hand, running it across my cheek. "I won't ever leave you." His hand drops to my chest, patting my heart. "I will live here, in the light we made."

Sobs rip through me. "No."

He coughs, and I can hear the death rattle. I pull out my phone, realizing I don't know the address. Desperation and defeat fight for the top spot in my heart. I push off him, turning and running outside. I get to the street, dialing 911.

The operator asks me questions, but I shout at her, "1901 Fairview Avenue. A man has been shot. He's a surgeon at a hospital in Seattle. He says it's a stomach wound and he's dying. Please hurry." She shouts things at me, but I run back inside, scrambling with my fingers to find light switches so the emergency workers can see their way inside. I hit something and a door opens. I hit something else and light flickers in the back. It's enough. I leave the door open and run to the flat. He's still breathing. I cling to him, holding my hand over the wound.

He opens one bloodshot eye. "Why are your hands so cold?"

It makes me smile through the sniffles and tears. "They're coming. I called for an ambulance. I told them you're a doctor from Seattle and that you've been shot."

He winces. "They're going to be looking for me. My blood is at the scene where Randall is dead. They're going to know I was hurt, and Rory knows I was a surgeon, doesn't he?"

I swallow hard, nodding after a moment.

"You have to run. You have to leave me here."

I shake my head but he pushes on me. "GO NOW!" His voice cracks.

I stand, backing away. "I can't leave you."

He pats his own chest. "You live in here. You can't leave me, ever. A person's heart can't be given away more than one time. After that it's not real. It's forced. I gave you my whole heart, and you gave me yours. We don't need anything else." The sirens in the distance change the subject for us. "Go, now. Go to the place you hid from the monsters."

I turn and run. I don't look back. I can't watch him die, and I can't stay and get caught too. Rory will win. Our best chance is with me free to kill him. I won't have any fancy way of doing it. I have only one way.

I take the car and drive as fast as I can to North Carolina. His cash is still in the car, thank God. I get some drive-thru food, suffer through it, and head for Pat's house just as the sun starts to come up. I have no way to contact Antoine, but I have to assume he isn't in on this. He's innocent and yet guilty by association. He will give my aunt to Rory and let him kill her but just not know that's what happened.

I park a block behind the house and run along the road, cutting through yards and hopping over fences, with a great deal of effort. I imagine it was the reason I stayed so skinny, to make running and hopping fences simple.

When I land on the grass with a thud in Pat's yard, I scan for any movement. I don't cut across the grass but hug the perimeter. There is a sedan parked out front. It's beige and has two guys in it. I almost roll my eyes.

I grab the hide-a-key from the planter and unlock the basement door. Slipping into the dark, I close the door and lock it. The shadows in the house remind me I'm scared of the dark. The ache in my heart reminds me I no longer care.

I hurry up the basement stairs, sneaking past the windows on the main floor and rushing the second-story stairs. I creep into Pat's room, pulling down the attic stairs inside her closet.

The light from the morning sun fills the attic. It's small and bright, with windows everywhere. I crawl up the stairs, pulling them up with me when I get inside. The space hasn't changed. There are still Barbie bins and coloring books. The dollhouse is dusty and smaller than I remember it being.

I glance about, wondering where I would have hidden something up here.

A fuzzy memory sneaks in, reminding me of the time I wrote a love letter to Dawson Diego. He gave it back with a big X across the spot where he had to pick yes or no. I saved all my tears and humiliation for this spot and then hid the letter behind the wall. I turn, seeing the very spot. You had to crawl across the ladder, and only a small child would be able to make it across. It was my very first booby trap. I scoot along the ladder, not sitting on it, but am able to reach across it to the spot where the panel pushes back with ease. Clearly I never clued into the fact adults have long arms . . .

I pull a large manila envelope from the panel. It's stuffed sort of full for something that should contain only a key.

When I open it up there is a ton of paperwork inside, all written in handwriting I don't recognize. I don't know what it means, but I'm guessing if I hid it, it must be important. I dig farther down, finding a key that looks nothing like a key. It's got the handle part, but the end looks like it belongs inside a computer. I think it's a high-tech key. It probably has a microchip in it—spies always say the word *microchip* like it means something. I honestly can't say what a microchip is. I don't even care slightly.

At the very bottom there is a letter. It's written in my handwriting.

I don't know who to address this to. I don't know who will find it. A me in the future, perhaps.

My name is Andrea Olson. I have discovered my name is actually Samantha Barnes. Anyone who knows me dies. Everyone who loves me is lying. I have to write this to you because I am about to lose my memories again. Whatever you do, don't fall for that one.

Trust no one. I made that mistake already.

There is a safe-deposit box in Turin, Italy, with some evidence in it. I went there, and before I could even get the box opened, a man tried to kill me. Something terrible is happening to me. I am covered in scars, and I don't know who I am. There's also a man chasing me. He says his name is Rory and he used to be my lover, but I don't believe him. He makes my skin crawl. He keeps asking me to take him to my father's house. If he did love me he would never ask that. Whatever you do, don't tell anyone when you leave for the security box. Just go there alone. I made the mistake of trusting Simon, my boyfriend. He's a liar too, and I don't think his name is Simon. I think it's Benjamin Dash, but I'm not sure. Whatever is in that box, he wants it. So does

Rory. I wanted to find it and destroy it, so I could be free of them all.

I have no advice for you except to go and destroy what's in that box. I have lost this battle. I am here to say good-bye to my aunt, but she isn't here. I remember her and this house. I remember so many things that make no sense.

I hope you remember me!

I don't know what to think of it. Clearly I didn't get the whole story from Derek last time. I just panicked and went rogue.

The only intriguing part of the entire letter is that Rory and I have met before. He knew I was on the run with Derek? So his pretending to see me for the first time in years was all an act.

Of course it was. He acted so nonchalant when he met me. He didn't run to me and hug me. He entered that office and was as cool as a cucumber. He was expecting me to be alive. He was expecting me to be with Derek.

I feel like I have more questions than anything. But I have one answer that I didn't before. I need to go to the safe-deposit box alone. I contemplate opening the ladder and climbing down that way, but there's a bad feeling inside me. My eyes glance at the window I always left from. It's awfully high up, but I know I've done it many times.

Deciding it's better to be scared of heights than it is to be caught by the two men in the sedan out front, I open the back window to the attic and climb onto the roof. Clinging to the envelope, I refuse to look anywhere but the place my feet have to go. I hurry down the back roof, hopping the two feet down onto the awning over the back deck. From there I walk to the end of it and jump. My feet tingle from the four-foot jump, and I could throw up if I gave it a second thought, but my heart is racing. I have brought the magical key of doom into the real world. The key everyone wants is right here in my hand. If I get caught, Derek and I are screwed. If Derek gets it, I don't know what he will do.

I hurry through the yards back to the car, fighting the terrible feeling I have that I am making a giant fucking mistake.

Getting to Italy isn't hard. Getting out of the United States without Rory finding me is. I use the passport and credit card Derek gave me when we were going to Austria.

I choose JFK as my airport, assuming it's so busy they won't be looking for me there. I catch the red-eye out, completely exhausted and, oddly enough, comfortable with sleeping on a jetliner.

When we land my eyes are aching, my heart is broken into a thousand pieces, and my mind doesn't stop wandering. But I drag myself from my seat and stumble down the aisle. Flight attendants smile and greet me, but I don't give a rat's ass about a single thing in the world. Derek is either dead or dying or sick. Binx is in a kennel, and he only ever lasts about a week. So I am on borrowed time with that one. Angie might be in danger. Pat is in danger. And whatever the hell is in that safety-deposit box is a risk I can't afford anymore.

A man ahead of me has his iPhone hanging from his bag. I walk closer to him, wiggling my fingers and watching the phone. It's a crazy idea but I reach up, slipping it from the bag, nudging him as I pocket it. He looks back, and I offer a sheepish grin. "Sorry."

When I get to customs in Rome, I smile and nod, hoping everything checks out for my new identity, Inga Deloncrae. My passport identity is an American from Maine. The man at the counter grants the seven days I require to attend the "business meeting" I am en route to Turin for. Italian men are easy when you smile and bat your eyelashes.

Once I've arrived in Turin, I am desperate to get back to the US. The cab ride from the small airport in Turin is short. I can't nap alone with a man I don't know, but my eyes are burning, almost as badly as my stomach is aching. I need food.

The aching and irritability don't end as we pull up outside of an unostentatious building. I have never seen a bank look like this before. It's stone and glass and might have been fancy once upon a time, but the area seems to have become laden in graffiti and cars I wouldn't assume were Italian. They're definitely not Lambos.

The cabbie leans back, giving me a smarmy look. I slap cash into his hand, not certain how much I've given him, but by the smile it must be an all-right amount. That was the only perk to stopping in Rome—I was able to change my money and clear customs.

I get out, gripping the key and watching the people on the streets. The sun is in the middle of the sky, but the air is cold. In the distance, snowcapped mountains surround the city. It's cold and blustery and not at all how I pictured Italy. I hurry up the steps, excited and anxious all at once.

When I get inside the marble foyer of the ancient-looking bank, warm air blasts me. I shiver with the chill I still have but walk to the front counter. A middle-aged and yet sensual-looking woman smiles at me. She asks in Italian if I have an appointment.

I shake my head, offering her Italian in return, to my own surprise. I explain that I just need to get into my safe-deposit box. She lifts a perfectly sculpted, dark eyebrow, explaining I will have to come back, as an appointment is necessary.

I nearly turn away, defeated and uncertain as to how long I will have to stay, when a man smiles wide, clapping his hands excitedly and rushing toward us. He embraces me, whispering in my ear in English, "Are you crazy?"

I nod against his cheek, almost relaxing into the scent of his aftershave. He smells like someone I know. He turns, telling the woman I am his special client, and drags me across the shiny stone floor to an office. When we are inside he offers a chair. "Ms. Barnes, I thought we agreed that you would never come here again."

I scowl. "I need to see inside the box."

His gaze narrows. "Why? No good can come of that. It's not an insurance policy if you take it out."

"I just want to look in on it, check its safety and ensure it's still intact." I know this dark-haired man. I know him, but I can't recall how.

He sits on the edge of the desk, looking down at me, sighing and nodding. "Fine, we go and look, and you leave. You never come back again. Your life is at risk just being here."

What the fuck?

Who the hell am I?

I know I was a spy once upon a time, but an Italian banker is worried about me? Needless to say, I am completely lost, and yet satisfied, when he opens the door again and leads me down the long hallway.

"We have to be very careful; keep your head down." He plucks my clothing. "At least you dressed incognito. No one here will recognize you."

We descend a wide set of stone stairs to the basement. They make me nervous with their sharp edges and brilliant shine. They're a deathtrap waiting to happen. I can feel my sneaker treads gripping the shiny floor, but he has on leather dress shoes. I'm terrified for him.

"They have been asking about you all over Europe. Searching high and low for three years. It's been painful to see them struggle." He's joking and mocking someone I don't know, but I smile and nod. He nudges me when we enter another corridor, this one much more glamorous looking. "You seem different."

"I am. I've had three years of peace and quiet."

He scoffs. "Right, like you and he could ever be peaceful."

The fact I don't know him or his name is driving me insane. I should have looked when we were in his office. A real spy would have looked. I am such a shopgirl.

He stops us at a giant room with frosted glass. "Do you have your key?"

I hesitate, almost not showing it to him, but the reality of the situation is that I must. So I lift it from my bra where I've been keeping it. He rolls his eyes. "Same Sam." He pulls a key from his pocket, and as he walks toward the room with the frosted glass, the doors swing open. In the dim light of the chandeliers and sconces and rich colors, a technology such as automatic doors seems off. We walk to a machine in the middle of the room. He holds his key at the opening on the right and nods at me, staring at the one on the left. I hold my key out as he counts down, "One, two, three." We push in at the same moment.

The machine sucks the keys in, keeping mine and then almost instantly pushing his back out. He takes it and nods at the door. "I will wait in the hallway." He leaves, and as he does, the doors lock with thick steel bolts.

I am trapped in a glass cage, and I have a feeling it's not the first time.

He stands with his back to the doors as the machine comes alive, clicking and grinding. It sounds medieval until a slot opens in the back wall and a large black metal box is placed on the single wooden desk.

I walk to it as the entire system sounds like it's doing everything it has just done in reverse.

My hands tremble. My heart races. My mouth dries completely as a threat of vomit attacks me. But I lift the lid, stepping back. I expect it is the Holy Grail inside. I expect light and fireworks. I expect to be wowed just by the sight of the greatness within this box. It is something to die for, after all.

But inside is a thick folder, something of a disappointment, I have to admit. It's huge, actually. I lift open the cover, scowling. "TOP SECRET" is stamped in red on the top of every page. Names are blacked out of some of it. JFK is mentioned on the second page, along with a man known as the Ruse. His name isn't mentioned but his deeds are. They call it an assignment—JFK was his assignment.

Oh shit. What do I have here?

I flip through, not understanding what all of this is until I reach the last couple of pages and find Derek. On these pages he is Dr. Benjamin Dash. My interest piques when I see his name repeatedly. The first couple of pages are what appears to be a doctor's report on "the incident," as they call it. A man was found dead, killed by venom from a snake not indigenous to the area they are in. Area Seven is what it is called. The person writing the report does not disclose what has transpired, but it appears Dr. Benjamin Dash's test subjects have been caught doing something unspeakable to fellow military personnel. The dead man's name was Dr. Andrew Holt, and an explanation is discussed, but it seems to be invented for the benefit of the deceased man's wife.

The next page is a summary by the doctor for the council. It doesn't explain the council or who they are.

Dr. Benjamin Dash has approved our test subjects. All seven have gone anywhere from twenty-five to thirty years without their disorders being discovered or diagnosed. They have never stood out as a problem and have managed their disabilities well enough to blend into regular society. For this reason we feel they will excel at the training. None are seriously disabled, the best to worst ranging from slight OCD to ADHD. In the beginning they were all forthcoming and up-front about all points of their prior lives. After only one week of training with Dr. Dash, the answers to the very same questions about the subjects' childhoods are suggestive and yet deliberately unhelpful. They are already showing signs of manipulation and overconfidence in areas where they have absolutely no expertise. Dr. Dash's theories on memory stimulation and the induction of psychosis in a person through false-memory stimulation are pioneering our ability to weaponize a person after they've moved to a country or become a useful asset through their career or ranking in society. The test results are the only reason we are continuing Dr. Dash's research. His ability to create the perfect agent through disassembling the brain and re-creating a weapon is unmatched in his field.

I feel the incident with Dr. Holt is not something that will repeat. Dr. Dash's control over the subjects has proven itself through exercises in which he is able to command them even as they are under the influence of the memory stimulation. We have approved seven of our own personnel to work with him in this study. All documentation will be Top Security Clearance, Level S. This shall further be known as Area Seven. Our hopes for the area are growth in the use of memory stimulation in sedated or deceased patients. We wish to unlock the secrets many try to take to the grave with them. The tests we are running are giving us the results we need to be hopeful that this is indeed a possible outcome for the project.

Regards,

Dr. Jenner Piscapault

There is a date stamp on it, but it doesn't make sense. It's only one year old. It would suggest I was here a year ago, which is impossible, considering I haven't been out of Seattle in a year, apart from now. Someone else has a key? Is that possible? It doesn't seem likely, considering the security here and level of friendship I clearly have with the man outside the door. I shake it off, pushing past the information. I need more answers than this. This has only raised questions.

Next I find an evaluation by the very same Dr. Jenner Piscapault. His write-up is technical, but from what I can comprehend, he is the psychiatrist in charge of determining a test subject's mental health. The assessment is tricky to understand; words like *diminished empathy*, *abnormal personality dimensions*, *disinhibition*, and *high psychoticism* stand out as the most used. I'm not the sharpest tool in the shed, but I understand the gist of it. The subject is a psycho, it's fairly obvious. They don't use the word, maybe afraid of labeling him or her. Or maybe all the words they keep repeating just mean *psycho*. I don't know, but I can tell they aren't the sort of words a person wants to have written about oneself.

Well, apart from one bit in the evaluation. The doctor found that test subject seven had remarkably low levels of narcissism for someone with such a lack of remorse or guilt.

> She has a strong connection to animals. She refuses to kill them when she's awake. The trauma from her childhood has stuck with her, and created psychosis. She sleepwalks, killing whatever comes into her path, even animals. When she wakes to find what she has done, the remorse returns. She cannot shake it when she discovers she has wronged an animal. She has become less attached to humans, though. She is the last test subject to assimilate to the cutting off of the emotional mind from the physical body. Permission has been granted to remove her from this test facility. She is to join him in a RL scenario testing. Dr. Angela O'Conner, from the United Kingdom, will be joining him. She specializes in this type of deep-cover, scenario-based training. It will be a controlled environment to further reach inside her.

My brain feels like it's about to explode, but the cracking sound inside my head is from my heart. Even if, apparently, I don't actually have one.

16. I WILL FREE YOU

The silence of the frosted-glass room is too much to endure when taking in knowledge such as this. I'm only about thirty percent sure I haven't actually fallen asleep and dreamt the things I am reading. I turn back, looking at the man with his back to the door, and wonder what he is to me, the real me. The man-made girl who believed a thousand lies and trusted her heart to a master puppeteer.

I am Pinocchio, only my blue fairy turned out to be a scheming bastard who wanted to make me an assassin. I blink again, staring at the words *expected date for reinsertion*, but I am drawing a blank as to what it means. The date is set for three months from today.

Three months?

I don't even think I can guess what it means, but I know it's bad. It's all bad. At the bottom of the box is a box of matches. I lift the folder with the random words, detailing things I won't ever understand, and feel the weight of it in my hands. It's heavy like a gun and a key and a secret are. It's heavy like it contains every secret in the world, every whisper of treachery.

But it doesn't. It contains only mine. Whispers of love and promises that he would take care of me.

I glance down into the bottom of the black metal bin, stunned when I see the words "I will free you." They're silver letters, scratched into the metal box.

One sentence.

I'm pretty sure I have an ulcer, and I'm positive this one sentence has flared it to a bad place. A place I might never heal from.

I turn, hurrying to the door, and bang on it.

He points at the box, shaking his head, and makes a weird motion with his hands. Clearly, he means I have to place the box back before the doors will open.

Of course . . .

I hurry back, stuffing the folder in the box and grabbing the box of matches. I don't know if I am making a terrible decision or if I am following the instincts that are inside me. I light the match and drop it into the papers. They light quickly, so I cover the box slightly, only letting a bit of air into it. Smoke starts to billow, making me promptly regret doing it. I glance back, seeing the man, and wonder if he can tell I'm burning something. The smoke fills the room, making the frosted glass appear far more frosted than before.

I have to back away as the folder burns up; the smoke is too thick. I blink away the stinging in my eyes and hurry back to the box, pushing the lid down all the way and sliding it to the spot. The door opens on the back wall, pulling the box back into the wall.

I turn and look at the door as it opens. He points at the spot where my key slides from. I shake my head. "I don't need it anymore."

He winces in the smoke. "I gathered." He nods at the large black box next to me. "It's a burn box."

I shrug and follow him from the room. "How do I know you?"

He glances back at me, sighing. "Again?" I nod, making him wince. He holds a hand out to the right, not the hallway we came down. "Come this way." He offers me his arm. "You and I met five years ago when he was starting something he referred to as the escape hatch. He placed what he called an emergency file into the safety-deposit box and got two keys cut. One for you and one for him."

"Who are you? Are you a doctor involved in all this?"

He chuckles. "No, Sam. I'm a banker. I just know him because of some business a few years ago."

"Who am I?"

He shakes his head. "Someone who means a lot to that man."

"Do you have answers for me?"

He shakes his head. "But I have a bag, a satchel that he left here last year. It will get you to where you need to go to end all of this and find your way back." He leads me to the back door and enters a small office. He opens a filing cabinet and hands me a man's satchel. He steps toward me, hugging me. I don't know what to do about it all or what to do with it, but I don't fight him on the embrace. He pats my back and nods. "Run, Sam. Run as fast as you can."

"I feel like a contestant on a game show. I feel like everything is a maze and I'm running through it, trying to survive, but I don't get answers, only more questions. I'm running in circles, lost in the maze."

He pulls back, running a hand down my cheek. "I can't imagine how that must be. I am so sorry, but these are the only answers I have for you."

"Well, thanks for the satchel." I have to assume there's a bomb in it, or worse. That's just the way my life has been going lately . . .

When I climb the stairs he presses a switch, and I hear the doors unlocking so I can walk out into the alley next to the large stone bank.

I lean my back against the door and sigh. The trip has been a waste in so many ways and a disaster in others. I don't have any clear answers. I don't know what aspects of my life are true or false.

I don't know anything. Clinging to the satchel, I walk the alley to a small coffee shop. I go inside, walking straight to the bathroom, and close the door. Kneeling down, I lift the lid from the bag, and I'm confused by its contents. There are stacks of euros and several passports, each containing a birth certificate to a different country and a driver's license. There are three cell phones, all turned off completely. A set of keys on a key chain with a boat on it. The boat's name is *Thackeray Binx*. I don't know how I know that but I do. My insides twist, reminding me I need to go get my damned cat back. The final thing is a notebook. I open it, finding handwritten notes about progress reports and dream analyses. They're in my writing.

I close the bag, wondering how the hell I will ever get away from all of this. I turn on the three phones, but only the white one comes up as having messages. I turn off the other two and press the voice mail button. I enter the code that I always use, and of course it works.

"Hi, Jane, it's Derek. Meet me in Paris at the place you remember. All will be revealed then, if it's safe." I scowl at the phone, not recalling a single place until he says the words "I will set you free." Then an image bursts into my head of an explosion, freeing up space and burning away old images as if I am watching a picture burn slowly. The haze of memories, lies that tell me I remember who I am, starts to clear away. The images are confusing, of course, but also enlightening. Suddenly, I'm alone on a pier, watching a sunset. A man is next to me. He watches the sunset too, not looking at me. For some reason I can't clearly see his face.

"I killed the doctor," he says like he is telling me it's Thursday or he likes sandwiches. I nod, not caring that another man is dead. He turns. His face is still hazy, but I know his voice. "Dash is dead, and I'm going to set us free."

"What if you can't free us both?" My lips move without thought or understanding, because it's a dream.

"Then I'll sacrifice myself so you can get away."

I shake my head, but he grins and I can see the vampire tooth through the haze. I love his grin. It's so lopsided and odd. It's a lie, though. It's boyish and sweet, but he's a monster.

He's my monster.

He runs his hand over my cheek. "I am so glad I found you in the dark."

I nod, not caring that a tear is slipping down my cheek. I turn, as if purposely looking for something. There are padlocks everywhere on the bridge. They are locked to the railings and iron fencing along the bridge. There are so many I can't guess: one million locks?

The image fades away instantly.

I blink and realize real tears have run down my cheeks. Pulling out the French passport and slipping it into my pocket, I hurry to the front counter, grabbing a pastry and a coffee. My body is malnourished, but there is something else driving me on. I'm terrified it's love.

Getting a cab is simple. Getting a plane ticket at the airport would be even simpler, but deciding what to do with the bag of passports and cash is not as easy. I don't know what to do with them, but I would guess it's a poor idea to bring them on a plane.

Seeing the sign for a solution, I hurry to the car rental place across the way and decide to do the stupidest thing I can. The navigational map says it's a seven-hour drive. I know I can drive seven hours.

When I decide to turn my brain off and pretend the whole world isn't falling apart, the trip is pleasant. It's refreshing and new to be in Europe, even if, technically, it's not new to my body. My eyes are dazzled by the old buildings, the Alps, and many other sights, while my mind works out the story. Nothing I create with the mess of details they have given me makes anything resembling a plausible story.

When I arrive on the outskirts of Paris, the navigational system commands me in Italian to take an exit. I follow it through the streets as they get busier and more crowded. I park the car when the nice Italian male voice tells me I am three hundred meters to my destination. Climbing from the car I stretch and wince as blood starts to circulate through my body more efficiently. I follow the image of the map as I recall it until I recognize the Pont de l'Archevêché. The padlock bridge. I have been here before.

I don't know when I was here, and I am certain I won't ever know the truth of it, but the image of thousands of padlocks lining the bridge stuns me to a still silence. Overwhelming awe and an instant respect for love, even the lost and not yet found, fills me. There is nothing I have ever seen that will ever compare to this. The locks are a symbol of hope in a world where I swear there is none. This bridge is a symbol of all the love out there, proving there is so much more than I would have guessed.

I stroll to the exact spot in my odd memory and sit, staring at the Seine and the people walking on the street across from me. Seeing them makes me wonder if they're normal people or if they have a past of secrets, deceptions, and betrayals like me.

There is no way Derek is coming, but I have to surmise he's the one I am expecting. But his injuries were serious. He will be in a hospital for many weeks, if he made it at all. I don't know why but the thought of a world without him burns inside me. I should wish him dead. I should wish them all dead. But I find when my eyes are closed I wish they were here with me. I wish I weren't alone and afraid and living a web of lies.

"You came."

I turn, seeing the pale face of a very sick Derek. He is hunched and weak, evoking pity from me instantly. I jump up, forgetting the bag and the lies and the bullshit. "Are you okay?" I am grateful he's alive. I can't deny it, and I won't bother pretending.

He shakes his head. "Did you find everything I left you?"

"You're alive, Derek. How is that even possible?"

"I left it all there for you, hoping it would give you some closure." His voice shakes, and I can tell he's not better—not at all. He shuffles his feet on the old cement and sits down next to me, overlooking the Seine. "Did it make sense?"

I shake my head. "You left me a bag and a box that made everything more confusing."

He turns, stunned. "You didn't read the pages?"

"There were *hundreds* of pages. I skimmed and saw shit like *JFK* and *narcissism* and shit I didn't understand, and I panicked. I burned it all in the safety-deposit box, smoked out that room in the bank brutally, and ran."

"Why didn't you use the burn box?"

I sigh. "Why does everyone think I know anything that's going on?"

"Because you do. It's just stuck in the layers, and I'm trying to help you get it out." The water, the passersby, and the charming little bridge make it all surreal.

"I don't trust you, and I don't trust anything I feel or see. These people could all be part of it somehow."

He scoffs, wincing a little. "Well, I'm not that good."

"You're Doctor Dash. You can do anything."

He shakes his head. "You should have read the pages, Sam." His eyes are gray. I should have noticed it before. The green, the joy, is gone. Maybe from us both. "I'm not Dash. He's dead. I killed him." He sighs. "I killed him for you. It's the only way out."

"What?"

"I killed Ben—Dr. Dash. We were brothers. No one knew. He was the brilliant doctor, and I was the—other brother." He swallows hard. Something dawns on me, or just repairs itself in my mind.

"You were one of the patients?"

He nods. "I was." He licks his lips. "You and I were both subjects at Area Seven." He looks down at the concrete, and I can tell he's in terrible pain. There's a glow of sweat across his brow. "You were a marine with a case of ADD, but you managed it so well. Taking yoga and doing exercises to focus your brain. You had agreed to be part of the program because it was explained to you that we would be used as operatives and in the same situations as SEALs. You wanted that, badly. You were fit and feisty and organized. Your brain was sharp." The corners of his beautiful lips turn up. "The perfect candidate."

"What were you?" There is a storm brewing inside me, but I need to focus on something other than myself.

"I was a doctor, just a regular doctor in the field. I followed my brother into medicine, but I didn't think I had the patience for behavioral work or neurosciences. I had OCD, severe sometimes. I would fixate, almost like an autistic, but I could be talked down. Only my brother ever knew about it." His voice trails off, making it feel as though we are watching his story and not hearing it. I can see everything he says, and his tone is so calming. "They used us, highly efficient people with coping mechanisms already in place, to create a program. Area Seven was a start of something profound." Bitterness fills his face. "Then it all started. Isolation, hypnotism, exercises for inducing paranoia, detachment, and disassociation. The science behind it was genius, but the application was cruel."

My entire body shivers as if it recalls all of those things, but I don't.

"I killed Ben and took his place." He looks at me with passion. "I just wanted to get you out. I didn't know any other way. I didn't know how to save you, so I pretended to be Ben and took you to Seattle and explained that we were doing a training exercise to try to fix your inability to detach fully. Instead, I was leading you back, doing everything in reverse. I have been taking you through the exercises, one by one. Creating a new persona was the hardest. You were truly a blank slate. I programmed you to react to certain words so that pieces of memory would find their way back to you slowly. If it went too fast it could shut down your mind altogether. It had to be slow and steady, piece by piece. Otherwise, you could end up stuck in this world."

I lift a hand. "My father never molested those girls?"

He shakes his head. "You're an orphan. Your parents came to America from England when you were seven. They were a loving couple, adored you. They died in a fiery crash in California, and you grew up in an orphanage. It wasn't magical or anything to be excited about, but you were never harmed or tortured or made to be anything but a regular girl."

A sob escapes my lips as my hands cover my eyes. Relief and sorrow fill me. "How could you?" I rock, shaking and gripping myself. "How could you make me think that?"

"I didn't. It was there already, in your mind and waiting for the moment they needed you. Then they could activate you."

I sob harder, clutching to my face. "I wasn't in an accident?"

"No."

"Angie?"

"A doctor to ensure you were adapting to the life you were told about. Adapting to become the sleeper cell in whatever city they needed you to be in."

My heart breaks. "My aunt Pat?"

"An actress paid to be your aunt. She was told you were a victim of the life we made you believe you lived. She was paid to be your aunt and to participate in the therapy sessions you were undertaking."

"Oh God, oh God." I can't take any more. I get up, looking around. I don't know where to run. I don't know what to do.

"Sam, wait. There's more. Don't run yet."

I close my eyes, letting the whole of Paris spin around me in a violent circle, a vortex.

"There is a way back. The layers in your mind, the subconscious that has been manipulated, it can be healed, I think."

I scowl, dropping my hands. "To what end? You will give me back my memories of living in a fucking cell and being tortured and made into this—killing machine who can't actually kill anything." Hot tears blind me.

"It will take away the false walls built in your mind."

"How do you know?"

He shudders. "I did it on myself first. How do you think I remember meeting you in the dark?"

The words have no meaning to me.

"I love you, Sam."

"You don't know me." I turn and run. I know he can't follow; his injuries are too severe. People become a blur and direction becomes a circle I run, chasing after myself in many ways.

When I think I am nowhere and everywhere all at once, I stop, heaving against the brick wall of the old building next to me. I grip the bag he left me, the one with all my identities in it. Which one is real? Are any of them? Was I an orphan? Was I the perfect candidate because no one would miss me?

I sink onto my heels, leaning and deep breathing. My head feels like it might explode, but in my heart I want to know the truth. I have come this far in the rat race they have set me up with. I want to know who I am and who I was and how I got here. I want to separate the fact from the fiction.

I get up, and as I walk down the alley I open the map app on my phone. I use it to get back to the bridge, feeling defeated and stuck at the end of the road. I am only halfway when I hear his voice again. "Trust me, I swear I will make it all better."

I look up, seeing a red spot on his shirt where his wound has obviously opened. But he offers me a hand, ignoring his own wounds. I walk to him, feeling a weepy silence overpowering me. I don't take his hand; I don't trust him with that part of me.

We stroll the street to a dark car parked across from the bridge. He holds a hand out. I pause. "Who was Rory?"

"CIA. They all were. It was a full op for them. They didn't know that they were being used to run a scenario with you. They don't even know Pat is an actress. They think I am Dash, gone rogue with you."

It doesn't make sense. "Rory said we were together, we were partners once, we had a past."

He nods. "You were operational then. It was the first phase of the training. You were pulled into a special-run program, a branch off the tree that was Area Seven."

"Rory is one of us too?"

He nods. "Rory's final phase was to leave you to die in the burning house. Randall was one of the doctors in charge of the assignment. He was to Rory as I am to you, in charge of your file."

"Did we kill Randall?"

He nods.

"And the other man?"

He nods again. "No one but Rory and Antoine know you exist now. That's the beauty of a top-secret assignment—very few people are in the need to know."

"I don't know if you're lying to me."

He opens the door and smiles weakly. "You will."

When we get inside the car, a man drives us out of the city. He doesn't speak. None of us do. I should have run. I should have kept running. That thought eats away at the rest of my mind, becoming my entire obsession. Derek's hands grip his legs, like the pain of his wounds is too much for him to take.

"You need a doctor."

He shakes his head slowly, his eyes darting to the driver. "Just going to take a few weeks to heal fully."

The driver doesn't look back. He doesn't notice us. He takes an exit off the small highway we're on and ends up driving down a country road. Expecting to see random farms, I am surprised by the beautiful chalets, old stone mansions, and vineyards. It's amazing, even if it can't get my mind off the situation I am in.

He slows as we near a large stone arch. Part of me hopes we turn into the archway, and part thinks the opposite. Turning down a driveway toward an old mansion doesn't bode well for me getting my memories back. In fact, it seems likely something contrary to that will occur.

But he turns into the archway, making a lump form in my throat. I am going to be murdered or something worse. I have been tricked again. Well, if I'm honest I've been tricked again and again and again and again, and I have let myself be tricked.

When there are no options on who to trust, you trust the lesser evil. The castle-like mansion we come upon when we crest the hill makes me think I might not have chosen the lesser of my evils.

It's creepy, laden with moss, vines, and gargoyles. I hate gargoyles. I think I do, anyway.

Fuck it—who cares what I liked or hated before? I hate them now. They're creepy. And only creepy people would put them on their house. The French estate is creepy.

That's a bad sign . . .

When the driver stops the car I can't feel my legs. Fear has settled in deep. Derek takes my hand in his, squeezing tightly and pulling me through the door. When I get a good look at the driver my stomach starts to sink. He's familiar. All familiarity makes me nervous. It means the person has been part of the charade since at least midway.

Or is it now midway and the end is not actually ever going to come into sight? The fear that I will be on the dance floor for the rest of my life, dancing the same dance and twirling in the arms of these partners, is a very real fear.

I look up at the massive building, preparing for it to be the asylum they use to erase my mind. Or worse. Maybe it's the prison I have to stay in while they wait for my scenario training to start next time. Maybe they will just put me into my coma here. Maybe this is it. My heart starts to beat, echoing around in my empty body.

Derek drags me to the front door. It's politely done, but it's forceful enough for me to know I have to cooperate.

His side is bleeding still, but his grip is tight nonetheless. The huge wooden door opens as we draw near, revealing a wrinkled old man in a butler's suit and tie. He nods his head. "Doctor, ma'am, how lovely to see you both again."

Again?

His accent is English, not French. How odd. He closes the door after us. I pause, taking in the splendor and grandeur of the room. Everything is so large I don't really have anything to compare it to, to justify the size. It is just bigger than any room I have ever been in inside a home, which this clearly is. The ostentatious art, the arched doorways, the sweeping stairs, even the dog is huge. The giant hound—a wolfhound, I think—walks to me. He runs his face over my hands. I think we might know each other, and I don't want to offend him, so I scratch the places I think he might like—behind the ears and between the eyes.

The butler leads the way, directing us through the halls of the home that seems less and less likely to be an asylum. I can't deny that makes me feel better.

Derek's grip on my hand becomes part of my body. I don't feel like I am being held or protected or dragged. His hand and mine are meant to be.

I feel that in my heart, separate from everything else, we are meant to be.

The butler stops outside of a room with a tremendous amount of light flooding it. There is a wall of glass and many skylights in the ceiling. A sunroom, perhaps. A woman with gray hair and a wrinkled face to match the butler's awaits us. I know she expects us, because when her bright-blue eyes flicker to my face, they light up with recognition.

"Sam, how are you?" She is also English. She doesn't stand, but holds her hands out for me. "I was your friend once, Samantha Barnes." Her eyes are not the same shade—they are light blue and dark blue, like mine.

I don't release Derek's hand or run to her; I wait for it but it doesn't come. I do not know her face.

She swallows hard, wincing. "It's all right, my love."

I suck my air. I know those words. She called me those words, those names. *My love.* They make more sense in my head now, the accent. My skin crawls with shivers.

"Do you know me at all?"

I shake my head. "But you shouldn't be insulted—I remember almost nothing and everything, and the stories don't match in my head or on paper."

She laughs at that. "I have missed you, my love."

"Who are you?"

Her eyes sparkle. "Your grandmother, Emily Starling. I was your mother's mother, before the accident."

Of course, my real parents were killed in a car accident. And they were English. I recall that detail. I was alone in the world; apparently not as alone as Derek must have assumed. Unless he too has known my only living relative all this time.

She holds a hand toward a fancy floral couch. "Have a seat. We will take tea, Thomas."

The butler nods and leaves.

Derek releases my hand, making my skin cold instantly. "If I may excuse myself, Madame Starling, my injuries would stain the couches badly. I will tend to myself and see you both at dinner." He kisses my cheeks, whispering in my ear, "You are safe here." He slips from the room, leaving me.

I don't know where this game is going to take us. I sit on the couch, wishing it were slightly less firm.

"Your parents took our firm to America. They were so excited to become Americans and see the sights. They never realized how alone we were as a family, just the five of us."

"Five?"

She nods, taking a large black book from the shelf next to her, again not moving her lower body. I am scared she can't move it at all. She opens the book, placing it on the large glass table in front of her and flipping through a lifetime. It's my lifetime. My parents—they match the flickers in my head. I refuse to attach myself to the images of the dead. I do not know when this reality will be a lie.

"You were so small and so obstinate." She lifts her face, revealing a grin. "I suppose that's the reason you are still alive, though, isn't it?"

I shake my head. "I don't know."

"This was your sister, Jane. She was so sweet and calm. She was the girl every parent thought their child should be."

It's like being punched in the guts. She is my twin. We are identical, even the eyes.

"You were so spicy. I always called you sugar and spice; she was the sugar, and you were the spice." Her eyes are fixated on the pictures of the small girls with brown hair and blue eyes and peacoats like Paddington Bear. A tear rolls down her wrinkled cheek. It's slow and lonely, the only one she sheds.

"Where is she?"

Her face lifts. "Oh, my poor darling. She's dead. She died in the car accident. The one you nearly died in too."

"Three years ago?"

She shakes her head. "No, some time now." She narrows her gaze, thinking. "It's been seventeen years."

"What!"

She nods slowly, still lost in the movie she's so obviously watching in her head. It starts as a picture but grows into a moment with each photo. "It's why they wanted you."

"The government, you mean?"

"Yes." Her tone sinks. "They wanted to test memory stimulation on you, and then they wanted to use you as a candidate for something else. Derek hasn't explained it to me well. I don't like hearing about it." She adjusts herself in the chair, trying to get more comfortable, maybe. "You and your sister were best friends. What was that song you girls always sang again?" I shake my head but she nods. "You know it. The one about the bullets are made of blood."

I scowl, wondering how she could know about a song I was given by a doctor. Did I tell her about the song? Is this a trick? "I don't recall it." I lie, but I don't know why. She doesn't scare me, but her knowing the song does.

The butler brings in the tea, offering me a cup with a drop of cream first and finishing with lemon, just the way I like it. "Thank you." I take it, inhaling a deep gulp of the aroma and then the tea. It's the perfect temperature to drink. The smell and the taste attempt to bring a vision, but it flickers like a radio not quite on the station. The words are lost in the fizz. I sip again, noticing the way my grandmother takes her mug, placing it down without drinking any and leaning back a bit. She smiles at me. "Biscuit, my love?"

I blink three times, and suddenly it's there. I feel as if I've sat in a field and a cloud has landed atop me, blocking me in its bright fluff. My eyes don't see and my ears don't hear, but there are sounds and movements. They're inside me, dancing in my head and making me believe I see them.

I squeeze my hands, to grip the cup, but it's not there, none of it's there.

"Where did you hide the monsters, Sam?" The question whispers in my ear.

The answer is there. I know this question, even if it is coming from a place I don't recognize.

"Where did the monsters go?"

Black images flash in my eyes, jerking and moving quickly, like a lightning strike. One second it's there in my eyes and then it's gone, but the flash remains in my view.

My lips part. I don't know what to say but I speak anyway. "The monster was gone, and I went to look—to look—to look—to look." I am stuck there. Hot tears trickle down my cheeks. "I only wanted to look. But the pretties were gone. He took them so I followed." The words are a whisper. "I can't say the rest aloud or the monster will hear and he will strike all he sees. Sometimes I think he strikes even the pretties who aren't there anymore. He speaks and shouts like they're in the room with us, like they made him do it, but I don't see them. They hide from me." The world becomes a blend of shapes and colors, but my eyes won't let me see. "I went to look and he was gone so I followed."

"Where did you follow the pretties, Sam?"

I shake my head, swearing I feel the sting of a lash against my skin. It makes me jerk, my back straightening harshly.

"If you tell us we will let you see them again."

I want that. I do. "I rode my bike to the water—the lake. It took me all day. I was hot and dusty. He was gone, on the boat with the pretties. But they were different." I shake my head, forcing the image of the blue wrapping from my mind. "They were different and then they were gone, to swim without me in the blue."

"The blue water, Sam? Were they like mermaids?"

I shudder. "The blue wrap. They were in the blue wrap, and they wouldn't talk to me anymore. They were different, and I was the same."

"Tell me about the swans, the way the swans circle the stars and the clouds shoot across the sky."

The words bring a type of calm with them. I can see the swans circling the stars. I don't know it at first. I blink in the sitting room, realizing I am alone. Derek walks in; his shirt is clean again. He smiles and drops to his knees, taking my hands in his and kissing them. He lifts my face, kissing me softly and muttering against my lips with hot breath, "I found you in the dark, and you became my light."

He kisses and fades away.

17. ALL THE PRETTIES IN A ROW

Can you hear my voice?" I can, but I cannot respond. There's a block, and my lips don't work. Light starts to poke its way through my lashes, beckoning me to come to the surface. "Come back, Jane. Come back to me." I think my lips crack a smile when I hear his voice.

I blink, trying desperately to let the light in. It blinds and shocks my eyes, but I push past the pain until I see something, a shape in the hazy fog. I blink it away like windshield wipers cleaning the mud off. He stands at the foot of the bed, giving me a look. I cock an eyebrow, moaning and trying to move my head a little. He sighs as if he's waited all day for this. "You all right?"

I lift my hand to my head, rubbing it. Everything is washing in, hitting me like waves after a storm. He sits on the bed, rubbing my foot as his face makes a story. He's Rory, my partner. "You had me worried this time; you were gone a long time."

I nod, finally sitting up a bit. "Lakes surrounding the house in Geneva. She rode her bike all day, but it couldn't be too far. She was eight, she couldn't have ridden too far." He's gone instantly, leaving me lying next to the blonde girl named Sam Barnes. She's still, peaceful looking, not at all how she seemed in her head. In there she was scared and unsure. I can feel it still on me, like I too am unsure of things. I wish I could take it away, all her memories—wash us both clean.

I wish I could go inside them and walk away scot-free, taking with me the evil they know so they can go in peace. But I can't. I take things away with me, things like songs and habits and fears, and sometimes they become mine too.

Rory comes in, grinning at me from ear to ear. "They've been dispatched. You're a fucking genius. We'll know something soon enough. There are seventeen lakes it could have been, but we cross-referenced with her father's friends to check on lakes he frequented or ones he avoided. The teams are dispatched."

"Stop cussing. It just gives Angie a reason to mock you."

He winks. "She loves me and she knows it, filthy mouth and all. Ya should hear her at home, cussing away like a typical Scot."

"You people are sick." I nod, not taking my eyes from Samantha Barnes's calm face. "It would have been a place he went to. Somewhere he wanted everyone to go to—he is smug."

"What?"

"The lake. He would have gone there, knowing they were dead and at the bottom of the lake. He would have reveled in it." I sit up completely, letting my legs fall from the bed.

Rory gives me his arm. "Take it easy, Jane. Ya get that Scotswoman angry and it's my arse later."

"You like her angry." I push off from the bed, falling forward and refusing his arm. I don't like it when he touches me. I have a hard time looking in his eyes and not seeing the way I think about him when I'm inside them. In their heads it's safe to look into his eyes and imagine what it must be like to be loved by something that harsh and rugged.

I land on the edge of her bed, staring at her pale lips. I can see them holding a cherry, just like her babysitter taught her to. I wish her eyes would open, and I wish her lips would speak to me. Instead, they will haunt me like the others. Too pale and too calm. No animation or life. She is alone inside that place now. She is still sitting on the floral couch in the house in France, the estate I visited once to make a place for my imaginary grandmother.

That's how it works. For as much as they let me inside their heads, I let them inside mine.

She is number seven for me. The seventh person I have entered and manipulated. The seventh person I have controlled and convinced to give me all their secrets, at the same time I let her see mine. There's always a moment when I glance at the glass and wish I could be the doctor behind the glass, observing. Maybe then my head wouldn't hurt quite as much as it does now, a leftover from the haze we make of each other's lives. But that moment is fleeting as the pain fades away and the reality of the insane act I have just committed settles in.

"She looks so young and sweet. I wouldn't have thought it possible for her to be like her father," Rory mutters, sounding like he finally sees her.

I shake my head. "She doesn't know she is. She doesn't know what she does when she sleeps. She remembers nothing. She believes herself to be a victim of him. When she thought she'd done something wrong it nearly killed her." I run my weak and trembling hand through her silky blonde hair. "She's not bad, not on purpose."

He lifts me back from the bed, helping me from the room. I don't look back. That was the last look I should take. I need to separate us now. I need to be me again.

When we are in the hallway Rory sighs again. "Are you sure you're all right? Ya look a bit pale." His thick Irish accent always makes me smile.

"I'm fine. Stop." But he's not the only one attacking me. As usual, Dr. Angie comes running from the viewing and monitoring room. "Och, lass. Ya shouldn't be outta that room just yet. Ya know I hate it when ya do that. Ror, ya need to be on top of this. You're supposed to be in the room until we clear her."

"She's meaner than she looks, Ang."

She glowers at him. "Ya wee chicken, letting a small girl boss ya around." She winks at me. We both know what kind of small girl I am.

Rory points at the chair. "I'll wait out here." I nod and let her take me in her arms. I don't need the help, but I have to humor her or she starts cussing and soon I'm no better than all the other bloody Yanks who annoy the piss outta her or the friggin' leprechaun she lives with. She's a bit racist, but she sounds funny when she does it, so everyone lets it slide.

She leads me to a chair, quickly checking my eyes and listening to my heart. I breathe several times as hard as I can, in and out. She sits next to me, shaking her head. "No more, Jane. Seven is more than anyone else."

I sigh, letting her put her fingers on my neck and arms. "I just wish I could fill the gap, you know?"

She shakes her head again. "No, I don't. But I'm not missing most of my life." She smiles, giving me that sweet face she always does.

It's then that he walks in, offering me a sweet smile. His lop-sided lips make me cringe inwardly. I recall every caress and every moment of them brushing against me. I know I blush every time I see the man, but I can't help it. I know I shouldn't use people I know when I slide into the minds of the criminals or patients, but I can't help it. Something real brings me back easier, and more whole than a made-up story.

Dr. Dash nods at me. "How was it?" His gray-green eyes fix on me, more gray than normal. He must be upset about something.

I shrug, desperate to seem cool and casual. If only he knew about the things I imagined he has done. "I found it, the spot. It was a lake. He wrapped the little girls in blue tarps and sunk them to the bottom of a lake."

"Jesus." That's his version of swearing. He's akin to a saint, but when he gets really worked up, that's it, he says *Jesus* or *what the hell*. I try not to say *motherfucker* or *twat* or any of the others my Irish partner and I chant regularly.

Dr. Dash shakes his head, mystified. I can see it on his face. "How long has she taken up after her father?"

"Since she was nine or ten, I think, but it was animals then, and no one knew. Her aunt came and took her away during her father's trial, abducted her from the state house she was always running away from. She lived in North Carolina and then went to university, but she never finished, so she worked in a shop. She started killing people three years ago when her father was released from jail."

"He was released after such a short amount of time?"

I nod. "Molestation charges were all they had on him. The disappearing girls were never seen at his residence. Everyone believed he did it, but they never proved a thing. When he got out, she went crazy. She went, from what I can understand, and tortured him. Then she killed him and stayed at that horrid old house. She lived like he was still alive, afraid of him. She would bring him the little girls like she did when she was a kid. He used her to lure them. She would take them back to his house, and they would dress up in pretty dresses and play. Last week she burnt the house to the ground when she woke covered in blood again."

He holds a hand up. "I can't do any more, Jane. Sorry. I don't know how you live with that in your head."

I lift my gaze to his. "I take things in there with me, things that will create a better memory than the ones the patients try to give me."

"That's actually genius." He swallows, looking as if he might get sick. My skin is prickled from the sickness of it all, but I don't let it be bigger in my mind than the image of him kissing me and holding me.

The door opens. "They got something. Let's ride." Rory nods at the hallway. I hop off the bed, fighting the dizziness. Dr. Dash grabs my arm, steadying me. I linger, feigning just how dizzy I actually am so I might stay in his grip a second longer. He smiles. "Maybe you should stay."

I shake my head. "I've been living in her head for the equivalent of a solid week. I need to see this to the end."

Rory kisses Angie on the cheek, remaining for a second to whisper something that earns him a wicked grin and a swat. She shakes her head at me. "I don't know how you spend hours in a car alone with him."

"He talks about you the whole time. It's not so bad." I wink at her and turn away.

He nudges me, glaring down. "Ya might keep some of those things to yourself. What happens on stakeout, stays on stakeout. Ya got me looking weak like a nancy to her. She won't respect me for that."

I chuckle, completely aware of the way their relationship works. "You like it when she disrespects you."

He nods. "Aye, I do." He opens the door to the roof when we get up the last flight of stairs. I remember the fear of heights and flying that came from Samantha Barnes and grin, refusing to let it get to me. "I'll drive."

He looks like he's about to argue, but he doesn't. He knows the things I take with me sometimes mess with my abilities at work. No one else knows. Turning on the engines, I sigh and let it all wash away. I have to conquer her fears in order to be rid of them. My palms sweat and my heart races, but I force it, lifting the helicopter into the air.

"How bad was it?" he finally asks when we are halfway to Geneva, Alabama.

"Bad. He used her to lure the girls, treated her like garbage, and locked her away under the house with a notch hole to watch everything he did. He whipped her when he caught her touching herself. That's those marks on her back. He whipped her until she was unconscious."

He blows his breath in disgust. "No bloody wonder she tried to kill herself."

I nod, hating the fact she is a monster because he treated her like one her whole life. Had she been born to a family who loved her, all those little girls would still be alive.

"Where did you leave her?"

That's the part that makes me smile. "With a new family in a beautiful home with a new memory."

He sighs again. "At least that's how she'll die, with a mind full of good things."

I don't want to talk about it anymore, and I can tell he doesn't either. We like the success, the closure. We dislike the thrill of the chase in their heads. He's done three. He does the men, and I do the women. If we suspect who they might be, we watch them, stalk them, and get evidence on them as best as we can. But if we don't know them at all, it's a hard ride in their mind. Samantha Barnes never popped up on our radar until a week ago when she slit her wrists in the concrete back room of her work. She sat there, bleeding out on the cold floor. Knowing who she was in the system made the right people curious, but her bedside confession to a nurse started this process. She fell into a coma before we could get any information. But luckily I don't need someone to be awake to give me everything they have.

I land the helicopter in a field near a police car. We hop out and run to it. My legs are shaky, but I force myself to be me, and I'm not scared of anything.

"We got the lake. It's bad. Over twenty so far. The entire state is there, I swear it. We've blocked out media, but they're trying to get in there." The local police officer gets the door for us. I climb in the back, letting Rory sit in the front with him. He's adorable; they always are. I love a man in uniform. My days in the military secured that in me.

"Are they dragging the lake?"

He nods. "Divers and dragging and five medical examiners. The FBI sent the forensics in. They've taken over the site."

Rory grins back at me, making me answer with an eye roll. "I'm not scared of the FBI."

The police officer chuckles. "Yeah, if I were you I wouldn't be either. Whoever you are, the entire site has been told to let you in and give you everything you ask for."

I nod. "Excellent."

He looks worried. "My boss told me if you asked for my virginity I was to give that up."

Rory and I both chuckle at his reddened cheeks. "I mean, I'm not a virgin."

Rory slaps him on the arm. "Your secret is safe with us."

The officer laughs, but I can tell he wishes he hadn't told us that detail. We make people nervous—uncategorized military personnel with a higher security clearance than the head of the CIA make everyone nervous. But we don't belong to the United States; we belong to everyone. A joint task force of nations with everyone from Interpol to the UN at our disposal for information and assistance.

We make people nervous. If they knew what we could do, they would be far more than scared. No one wants to know a person can crawl inside them, rifling through their secrets.

He drives us down a dusty road through the woods.

She was hot and dusty when she came down this road. He turns at a spot I wouldn't have. The road looks rugged. When he stops I am stunned. It takes a lot to surprise me, but the lake is shockingly beautiful. It's not how I pictured it. I never saw it in her head, but I wish I had. It would be more beautiful without the mass of law enforcement and medical staff everywhere.

We jump out, running immediately for the line of blue tarps on the side of the rocky beach. I pause, shaking my head when I see them all lined up. There are over twenty now. Rory stands next to me, whistling. "You hit the fucking jackpot."

"Stop cussing." My words are blank, but my heart is aching. The pretties who are different, who didn't talk anymore or look at her, line the beach, each one tied with rope in varying states of decay.

A man in a white forensics suit comes walking over. His face is gray, and his eyes are heavy. "Quite the tip you got there. Can't say I ever saw this many bodies in one place."

I nod. What else is there to say? I have seen this many bodies before. I have seen them in Italy—Turin, to be exact. They never lined a beautiful shore. They lined a bunker in the hills, and they weren't corpses any longer. They were skeletons. I glance up at Rory, wondering if he is reliving the events from that place. His haunted eyes suggest he might be.

18. THE BACKSTORY

When I walk into my town house the black-and-white fiend who stalks the halls comes running. I lift him up, taking a deep inhale of him with my eyes closed. "I missed you too, Binxy." He purrs, rubbing his head against mine. His thick fur tangles in my fingers, and I notice he's heavier. "Someone has been milking a certain nice old lady for treats."

He purrs innocently, ignoring my accusations. If it weren't for those treats he'd be clawing at me, so we are both grateful. He gets mean when he's alone too much.

I place him down, noticing the smell in the house. She's left me food again. Mrs. Starling is the best neighbor a girl could have. She bakes and cooks and cares for my cat when I'm away. Her children live all the way in Seattle, running the family company there. She's alone in DC, like me. We make for the very best neighbors. She likes to give, even when you don't ask, and I like to pretend we are family. She is the one person in the world I have. I take the dish of piping-hot chicken Parmesan, my favorite, out of the oven, and start to heat up the noodles in the microwave. Leaning over the top I smell the spices and herbs mixing with the cheese and sauce. It's a perfect food, really.

There's a knock at the door, interrupting my worshipping.

I turn, sketchy for a second, but then I remember I am not Samantha Barnes and walk to the door, lifting Binx up so he doesn't run away. I nearly gasp when I see the green/gray eyes staring down on me. He lifts my lipstick-red bag into the air. "You forgot this."

"Thank you." I take it from him, trying not to imagine us writhing against one another, trying not to be obvious that I am in love with him. He glances down, his glasses and fluffy hair making me smile. There's no way they can hide the perfection of his face and expressions. He's a Clark Kent.

He looks behind him at his silver Mercedes in my driveway. "Well, I guess I'll see you tomorrow."

I point behind me, mimicking him, and blurting, "I have dinner prepared. Do you want to come in?"

"I'd love to." He nods, saying it too quickly. "What did you make?"

My cheeks light up. "Oh, I don't cook. My neighbor cooks, but she's diabetic and can't eat much of anything she makes, so she leaves it here. She knows I eat like a horse." I'm an idiot. I can take down an entire cartel alone and sharpshoot like I invented it, but I can't talk to him without saying ridiculous things.

He grins. "I like girls who eat." He scowls, and I imagine we are suddenly on the same page, the uncool page. He clearly regrets saying it and tries to fix it. "I mean, instead of girls who pretend they don't eat, or go to the bathroom. You know, they always look too perfect, too skinny."

It makes me laugh as he somehow ends up digging a larger hole. "I know what you mean." I step back, letting him come into my town house.

He closes the door, leaning against it and smelling the air around us. "Wow, what is that? Chicken Parmesan?"

I nod, mystified at his ability to smell things and guess so accurately. I thought only I could do it. "Yeah, she knows it's my favorite."

He nods. "I love it. My mom always makes it extra saucy so I can drag my bread through it."

I nod. "I know. We had this conversation once."

He smiles, making me lightheaded. "Right, of course we did." I turn. I don't want him to see me faint, and I don't want to gawk, so turning away is the safest option. I grab plates, not sure what to say. At work we talk about work things, and here I don't want to do that. But I know everything about him. Asking questions about things I know would seem stupid.

"You must be excited the whole Samantha Barnes thing is over." He goes for the safe option.

"I am. I can't believe what it turned into—what a nightmare it was."

"Are you upset they're pulling the plug tomorrow?"

I shake my head. "No. She needs to be free. That's the only way." I don't want to talk about it anymore, so I don't say anything further on it.

I dish us both up a heaping serving of chicken Parm over the noodles from the microwave. Mrs. Starling hates that I heat them up in there, but I don't care. I eat from a box most days. "Do you want to pick wine?" I point at the wine rack in the corner. "It's all red; I'm a picky wino. I never drink white."

"It wouldn't go with chicken Parm anyway. Wow, what a great selection. You must pick up some wine for me next time you're in an amazing foreign country. You can't get any of these here."

It makes me smile, like a moron, but I can't fight it. I want to buy him wine and make him dinner and see him smile. I want his hands to brush against my cheeks. My stomach aches for it as if my body truly remembers his touches. "I would be happy to. Or you could just come next time, see some of the world. It's pretty impressive out there. And we can smuggle as much wine as we want, no pesky customs to deal with."

He glances at me. "I would like that."

I carry the plates to the table, noticing the way Binx is rubbing against his ankles. My fingers reach up and pinch my arm, but he's still there, and my cat is still loving him. He grabs a bottle as I grab the opener and glasses. He opens and pours, giving me a longing stare. I am trapped in his green eyes. The gray is almost all gone. The awkwardness is heavy, but I don't care. It feels like a now-or-never moment. I need to try to tell him how I feel and what I want.

"I like you, Jane." He beats me to it.

There are a thousand words I want to say, but I don't. I sit there like a complete douche and stare. It's like he's read my mind.

"I have to confess something. It's weighing a ton on my chest, and I don't think I'll ever have the balls to do it if I don't do it now." He looks into my eyes. "I saw inside your file, the one with the triggers and memories you fabricated to take with you. When you said something earlier about how you take things with you, I looked in your personal file to see what your triggers were."

Nope, he read my file. That's so much worse. My insides tighten. Fuck! He's seen behind the curtain. He's seen my creation of Derek, his alter ego who loves me.

He sits, taking the wine he's poured and handing me a glass and lifting his. "I just wanted you to know, I looked because I was hoping for some insight into asking a girl like you out."

My cheeks are on fire from imagining him rooting through my bag—not that I have anything in there, but still.

"I crossed a line, and I know that, but I'm not sorry. I like you, a lot."

I swallow, lifting my glass to join his. "I don't know what to say." It dawns on me I am scared of him. He is the only thing I fear. He is the type of monster that scares me. He's the kind you marry and you love forever. He's the kind who breaks everything inside you when they die and leave you, so it's better not to be with one of them. One of those real monsters.

"Say you'll go out with me and you like me back and that you wish I'd kept my greasy fingers off your personal shit. Say you wished I hadn't stolen your handbag so I had a reason to come over and that you would like me to leave because I am an asshole for being so manipulative."

I shake my head, whispering, "You swore."

He smiles. "I swear all the time."

"You never swear. You say *Jesus*, but it's more like you're praying. And you say other Ned Flanders–like swear words. *Gosh diddly dang* and all of that."

He cocks an eyebrow. "I do not. Who's Ned?"

"From *The Simpsons*." I roll my eyes, clicking my glass against his. "I like you back. Stay out of my personal shit, weirdo. I'm glad you stole my purse, and I'm happy you're here."

"Then we don't need to talk about it anymore?"

I shake my head, praying we never have to talk about it again. He drinks, but his eyes are fixed on me. I cut into my chicken, moaning at the perfection of Emily's cooking. He moans when he bites his too. "Who made this?"

"My neighbor. She's awesome. The only family I really have in the world."

He nods, savoring the flavors. "Tell me how you figured out that you needed to take positive memories in with you, even if they were fabricated."

He's the doctor behind the science so I tell him, even though I'm sure it won't be nearly as fascinating as he's hoping. And all it's going to do is make me look like a psycho. We both know I am, a little— I wouldn't have qualified for the program if I weren't. "When I got inside the first person's head, my life melded with theirs. I wasn't prepared to share so much with a stranger. I know you don't know me super well, but I don't like to share. I don't like talking about things. It makes me uncomfortable, but you can't go inside without giving something away. Seeing how sad my life was, little orphan Jane Doe, I created a new one. I got Angie to hypnotize me, but I never told her who the real people were who made up the memories. She knew she was my boss in all things. Rory was my partner. But Derek, the delightful doctor I created, was a mystery. I never told anyone who he was." I narrow my gaze. "How did you know it was you?"

He shakes his head. "I just did. I saw the description of him and knew. I'm from the East Coast but look like I'm from the West Coast. I'm a fitness freak, or whatever you called it. I'm always trying to stay positive. I drive a silver Mercedes." He glances down. "And I think you must have known, deep down, how I felt about you."

I swallow hard.

"You must have known subconsciously that I was in love with you." He looks scared of everything he's saying. I know I am. My heart races, and my mouth feels like it's stuffed with cotton balls.

He puts his fork down, no longer looking at me but instead at the table in front of him. He swallows hard like I do and nods, looking brave. That's the word I would use, *brave.* "When you're under, I always talk to you, hoping I can reach you on another level and make you see that we should be together." He sighs. "And now I look like I should be the person on the table, not the doctor." He lifts his face, pleading with his stare. "I swear, I'm not some creepy pervert."

"I know everything there is to know about you. I know you aren't a pervert." I reach across the table, doing the thing I think I have always wanted to do, and take his hand in mine. I need to be brave like him. "You are the thing that gets me through. I think I hear your voice and know I'm okay. Somehow, you're able to find me in the dark and make it light for me."

"Please don't ever go back in." He nods, looking at me. "I hate what I made you do. I hate that you go in there and use science I let the military force down your throat. I don't want you to go in anymore."

I squeeze his warm hand, sending chills up my own spine. "I won't. I won't go back in unless it's an emergency. Angie says seven is a lot. But you should know, you didn't make me become what I am. I might have been a candidate in the beginning, but I could have walked away and declined the offer. No one can make me do anything. That's how I ended up here. I'm a survivor."

He smiles, and the air clears of the heaviness around us. "I know you are. I know everything about you too. That's sort of the problem being us, isn't it? There might actually be such a thing as knowing too much."

"No, I like that there are no secrets. I don't like secrets."

He squeezes my hand back. "I know that too." He lifts my hand to his lips, pressing his warm mouth to my skin. We sit, frozen this way for a second, not moving but trembling with the next ten steps we both already have planned out.

The moment I move he does too. As I jump up he grabs my body. Nothing is the way I have imagined. It's better. Our lips slide against one another, our tongues seeking out the loving caress of each other. His hands are firm, rough even. He slams me into a wall; my legs wrap around his waist as he kisses along my neck and cheek until he reaches my mouth. Everything is better. His lips taste like wine, but he kisses in a way that makes butterflies dance inside me. Our hands move in rhythm made by our hearts beating against each other. He lifts me again, carrying me down the hall. I grip him, nodding with my face as he kisses my neck. "This room here."

He carries me in, laying me back on the bed. I can tell he wants to look down at me and appreciate the moment, but I grab his shirt and drag him down onto my comforter covered in pink roses, my favorite.

The light from the hall is enough to see his body is far better than I imagined it to be. We are naked and writhing against each other, just as I always wished we would.

There is no way I could have been more wrong about every aspect of him. When he's on top of me, pushing himself inside, I swear I have never felt anything like it. He doesn't treat me like a gentle creature or pay homage; he's rough in the right way. He doesn't quite make love, and that's the way I like it. He thrusts, lifting my leg higher, so my calf rests upon his shoulder. It's a steady balance of thrust, pressure, and size, and it brings me to an orgasmic level of joy I couldn't dream of. We orgasm together, collapsing in a heap of awkward sweat.

He kisses my cheek, whispering into the brush of our skin, "I don't know if I should apologize or thank you."

I smile. "Do either and I will murder you."

"And we can't forget you actually know how to do it and get away with it."

"That is a fact you don't want to overlook." I turn my face, brushing my lips against his. "Can we just be who we are in this room and forget everything else in the real world?"

He nods. "And make up some story about how we met. Something plain and normal like your cat got out and I found him and we fell in love at first glance?"

"That's a good story, but who do you plan on telling it to?"

"Just in case we need a backstory one day." He grins, and I feel it against my lips. His discussing a future "one day," after we've had sex for the first time ever, makes me moan, which in turn makes him laugh. "Did I scare you, Agent Spears? I know how much you like the possibility that one day you might be a normal girl."

I shove him back. "You're mean, going for my weaknesses like that." He ignores my whining and wraps himself around me. I feel his fingers find my scars in the dark. It's like telling him my secrets, but with him I never have to explain. I don't ever have to say the words *My entire family died in a terrible fiery crash.* I lived, but I lost them in every way. I lost my twin sister, Andrea. I lost my father and my mother. I lost everything in a blink of pain and screaming, but then in a secondary way, I lost them again. When I woke from the coma, after six months, I was a blank slate. I was alone in the world. I was an orphan of the truest kind.

A person can only lose so much before God or whatever force there is shines a light upon him or her. That light for me was an orphanage where I learned how to be me. I learned to be strong, because the nuns were strong. I learned how to be fast, because the mean kids at school were faster. I learned to be cruel in response to cruelty being inflicted upon me by kids from the town where the orphanage was. But I also learned there were comforts in the world, comforts you had to find. The sound of dishes and humming and singing and cooking. Those were good sounds. Rose gardens with pink roses everywhere—those were beautiful places to hide and be alone. Shredding paper in the head nun's office for fun was a comfort. The smell of shredded paper still makes me smile. The nuns loved us in their capacity and treated us with kindness and grace. They taught us to be good people.

When you lose everything, you are grateful for the little things you find.

His fingers tracing the scar where I lost the ability to ever have children is a little thing. He knows what the scar is, and yet he is making up a backstory to be with me. Maybe it's only in this moment, maybe it's for the rest of my life, maybe it's for a year. It doesn't matter, because to an orphan like me an hour like this one is something to cherish. And working with people like Samantha Barnes is perspective a person can always use. My parents loved me, I'm sure of that. I'm sure they never meant to leave me behind. And at the very least, they never harmed me. They never left me to kill myself in a concrete room out of desperation to stop myself from becoming them.

No, my parents and my twin sister were good people.

I close my eyes, grateful he is here, and let him be bigger than anything else in the world. And if we wake up in the morning and decide we don't need a backstory, I will be grateful we had tonight because it was more than I ever imagined.

EPILOGUE
A YEAR LATER

I creep into the town house, worried about what I might find. The smell is amazing, but it's silent. I tiptoe into the kitchen to find nothing but the oven on and some dishes in the sink. The table in the dining room is set, with wineglasses and a pink rose across my plate. The living room is empty, and Binx is nowhere to be seen. My heart is racing, my mouth is dry, and I'm not sure of exactly what to expect, but I know it's going to be bad. He's such a diva, drama queen, and emotional mess. I can't take it.

I almost turn and run from the house, but the sight of the engagement ring on my left hand makes me stop. I said yes. We made a plan, and I agreed to it. I can't run now. It's too late. And I don't want to anyway. The ring brings a grin to my lips.

I walk to the bedroom, feeling like I might faint or be sick any second. He's sitting in a chair in the corner, alone in the dark like Norman Bates. It's creepy, but I walk into the room anyway.

"You signed up to do a mind run in the girl they found in the river?"

I nod, even though it's dark and he probably can't see me.

"You promised you wouldn't do any more of them."

I nod again.

"The appropriate response is to argue back, Jane. Jesus." He says it like he's praying.

"I know that. I just don't really have an excuse. She's the girl who was missing from that college out west last spring, the eleventh girl on that case Rory was talking about. She's got defensive wounds, and she's been fed, but she's horribly pale. I don't know a college girl who lets her skin get that pale. She's escaped, and whoever had her is going to be looking for her. It's going to be a small run, I swear. I just need to know who keeps taking them."

"Why? Why can't you wait and see if she wakes up?"

I sit on the chair by the door, not crossing the room. He'll win the argument if he gets near me. He has skills I do not possess. "Because she might wake like me, forgetting everything. Or she might not wake, and he will worry that one of his girls got away. We haven't found a single body of the other ten girls. No one has turned up. He's keeping them alive and torturing them. I know it. When he panics because she's been found, he's going to purge and run, and we're going to lose him. We'll find the girls, but he'll be long gone."

He's silent. He knows I'm right. "I'll give you the day, that's it. Then I want your name out of the hat. No more mind runs."

I crack a grin at my success. "Lucky number eight."

He shakes his head. I barely catch it in the dark, but the annoyed sigh is obvious. I lift my left hand. "Still wearing the ring."

"It's been four hours." He clearly doesn't see how remarkable that is, so I go for the thing I've been holding back.

"I put in for a transfer. Into a profiling position that has no guns, stakeouts, or mind runs. Hardly any travel and no chance of me being killed in any small way, except from boredom."

He's up and out of the chair instantly. Even Binx crosses the room to me. Dash scoops me into his arms, kissing my neck. "That is amazing news. Military profiling—what a great job. I bet it even comes with a raise."

"Yeah," I sigh.

He laughs and carries me to the kitchen. "You are such a baby sometimes." I shrug as he places me down and pulls out my chair. "I made something new."

I wrinkle my nose. "I don't want new."

He rolls his green eyes. "You're getting new. We have to talk about the wedding."

"Just make it whatever you want. I don't honestly care."

His face drops, making me jump up and kiss him quickly. "I mean, I would elope. I don't have family or anything so it doesn't matter to me."

He kisses me back, but it's wooden. "Well, my mother is from Virginia. There is no way I am getting away with anything less than four hundred people. She's already insisted that if I don't bring you there for Christmas in a month I will be an orphan too."

I wince against his face. "Christmas?"

He nods. "It'll be great. You'll have fun. My sister is amazing, and my mother cooks like it was her profession."

"What was her profession?"

"Gossip and charities, mostly, but you'll be fine. She knows you don't have family and grew up in an orphanage. She knows you're not big on sharing or talking or hugging or—"

"I hug!"

"Your cat doesn't count."

I hug Dash harder. "I hug you, and Angie sometimes."

"Okay, I'll strike hugging from the list then." He makes me smile. He kisses my forehead, lingering to breathe me in the way I do Binx. "You don't have to do anything but be you. I don't care if she likes you or not. I love you, Jane Spears. I have loved you since the moment I first saw you."

I narrow my gaze. "In the room where we were doing interviews but really you were testing our mental capabilities?"

He laughs. "That's not the first time I saw you."

"What?"

He shakes his head, kissing my forehead and letting me go so he can grab dinner. He pulls it from the oven, making me suspicious as to what is in the large casserole dish. "No, the first time I saw you was in New York at the UN building. You were summoned to be a bodyguard to a visiting dignitary. You looked through me, like you never even saw me."

"What were you doing there?" I recall the duty, but not Dash.

He grins. "Your security clearance doesn't go that high."

I roll my eyes and take my seat. He places the dish down, taking the lid off slowly. I smile instantly when I see enchiladas from Emily next door. "You dick, I thought for sure you'd cooked up some kind of concoction."

"Not a chance. I got home, and she rushed them over. Gave me this lime mayonnaise to put on top of the sour cream." He grabs the dishes and sits across from me, his green eyes dazzling. "Now that I have your attention, I want you to swear to me that you will come to Virginia for Christmas."

I glance at the dish, fight the bursting smells attacking my nose with tempting scents, and look at the front door. He has me trapped. "Fine, I'll come."

He smiles wide, dishing me up two huge enchiladas. "She said you would be difficult when I told her."

"Who?" I lean over the plate, smelling the steam as he passes me the salsa and sour cream.

"Emily. I asked if she could take care of Binx while we went, and she laughed at me. She said taking you in was like slowly winning over a stray cat, and my mom would have better luck charming a python."

I grin, not insulted in the least. "See, she knows me at least."

He lifts his glass of sangria, forcing me to put down my fork and lift mine. "To you, my savage fiancée. I am so grateful you said yes."

"To Binx, for always being crabby unless he wants something." I scowl and lift my glass just a little higher.

Dash chuckles, giving me the lopsided grin. "You're a pain in the ass."

"I know, but you love me so you're sort of stuck with me."

He winks. "And your little cat too." I blink, realizing he's told a joke and I'm meant to be laughing. He sighs and takes a bite, moaning into his fork. "I don't care what you say all night, nothing can ruin this moment. You are wearing my ring, meeting my mother, and this food is ridiculous."

My evil stare-down doesn't last when I start eating. He grins at me from across the plate. "You glad we got a backstory now?"

I lift my middle finger into the air. "Shhhhh. Don't wreck this."

He shakes his head. "You're getting it after dinner."

I grin back, desperately hoping I am getting it. We both look down at my hand resting on the table. A goofy smile crosses his lips, forcing one across mine. He sighs, and I can see there is some kind of bliss going on behind those eyes and I'm the one who put it there. That has to be some sort of miracle. I took it each day at a time for a year and still ended up here, in a committed place where there is no doubt that one day we will be those golden-retriever people. We'll have a boxy SUV and a house with grass all around it. Because that's the sort of monster he is. The worst kind, really. I almost can't wait for tomorrow when I take a mind ride into that unconscious girl. I can't wait to free the other girls. It will be my last time doing something dangerous, my last trip down into the gutters.

And then I will try very hard to be like him. I suspect even if I can't be exactly like him, he won't care. I got one thing right about him in the mind rides where I created his alter ego. He has one tremendous trait in common with Derek, my made-up version of him. He will love me for who I am, because that's who he is. So if I only offer an inch, he'll take it and wait for me to give more. He's generous with his love and feelings, in an awkward way, and he's patient with me.

His eyes see through my grin. "Tomorrow I will be at your side the entire time, okay?"

I nod. Just a little bit excited.

We do dishes, flicking each other with soap and laughing as Binx earns himself a bubble cap. He paws and shakes until it's gone and then struts off indignantly.

We make love in our way that really has nothing to do with making love, but it works, especially in the dark where we aren't accountable for the things we want.

We go to bed.

It's the makings of a very beautiful life.

I sleep cocooned in him, safe from the world out there where we have to make choices and be strong.

When I wake, it takes a second for the haze to slip from my mind. I nearly forgot I was doing a mind ride today. I shower and get dressed into something comfortable. His eyes don't leave me, stalking me throughout the house. I know he's worried, but I'm not. When we arrive at work, he's tense. He gives me a peck on the cheek and whispers, "See you in the dark."

It makes me grin. I look back at him as I enter the room where the petite brunette is sleeping on the bed next to my vacant one. I offer a subtle wave and kiss.

"Don't forget your triggers."

It makes me smile wider. "Don't forget to tell your mom I like Italian food."

He scoffs, seeing how seriously I am taking everything. I close the door, looking at him through the glass. He waves and walks into his side of the room, behind the glass.

When I get inside I lift my left hand up to the glass. "Angie, look." I know she's screaming in the doctors' room. She's always shouting about everything.

Rory comes strolling in, closing the door behind him. His eyes find the ring. He nods. "Finally nailed you down then, eh?"

I shrug, lying back on the bed so he can sit down and we can start. Rory leans in, whispering, "Does he know just how long you've stalked his ass?"

"He does."

"Then I guess he's as crazy as you are." He sighs and looks over at the girl. "Who am I this time, Jane?"

I glance at her too. "My brother, Rory Hamilton. We're twins."

"Good idea; stick close to the storylines for our reality. Did you add some spy stuff to justify your natural skills and skepticism?"

"Yup." I fold my arms over my chest and lie back. He wraps me in tightly, sitting next to me, like he always does.

"Okay, work fast. We need to find where this nutbag is keeping these girls."

I glance up at him as he tucks me in snug as a bug in a rug, like his mother always did for him. "You know me, I like everything fast."

He winks. "Apart from love. The good doctor would agree to that, I'm sure."

I shake my head. "Don't get him started. He doesn't need encouraging."

Rory blows a kiss at the mirror. "Ahh, my sweet Angie had the same troubles as he does. She was chasing me all over hell's half acre, trying to nail me down."

"Oh my God, you're a dork. She's going to kick some ass later for that one."

His wicked grin matches the one she gets at times. "God help me, I hope so."

I close my eyes, grateful for everything and ready to help someone else find their freedom. Everything is a mess in the world I am about to enter, so having my world in order makes it easier.

I lie back, reminding myself of the triggers.

The purple scarf my mother was wearing when she died. I still have the picture of our family the day the accident happened. The purple scarf was so tight around her neck it still bothers me.

The wooden box with the four-leaf clover in the lid that I made with Andrea and Mom. I still have it.

The saying that my master chief always said in training. *Loss of love, loss of limb, and loss of life are all equal tragedies.* He was a genius.

Dash—or Derek, as I call him here so I don't confuse the two of them in real life—he's the light in the dark and the voice that brings me home.

Binx. The black-and-white cat who will forever have my heart.

Twins, because I once shared something with a person that can't ever be taken away from me, even in death—creation. I shared a womb, and I shared my life with a person who will always be with me.

Rory, because he always has my back and he's hot in a naughty way.

Angie, because she always makes me laugh.

Pink roses, because they're my favorite.

Shredded paper, because once upon a time that was the only solitude I had.

Noisy kitchens, because they remind me maybe I was an orphan but my life was still amazing. I had food and shelter and love and support.

And now the ring on my finger, because it means forever, and for the first time in my life that word makes sense.

I take deep breaths, ready to take on whatever this young girl named Ashley Potter has to throw at me.

Because I am a survivor.

DON'T MISS SIN AND SWOON, THE SECOND BOOK IN
THE BLOOD AND BONE SERIES BY TARA BROWN.

SUMMER 2015

ABOUT THE AUTHOR

Tara Brown writes in a variety of genres. In addition to her futuristic Born Trilogy stories and her nine-part Devil's Roses fantasy series, she has also published a number of popular contemporary and paranormal romances, science fiction novels, thrillers, and romantic comedies. She enjoys writing dark and moody tales involving strong, often female lead characters who are more prone to vanquishing evil than perpetrating it. She shares her home with her husband, two daughters, two cats, and a beagle.